THE SPANISH MILLIONAIRE'S RUNAWAY BRIDE

THE SPANISH MILLIONAIRE'S RUNAWAY BRIDE

SUSAN MEIER

MILLS & BOON

First published in Great Britain 2018
by Mills & Boon, an imprint of HarperCollins*Publishers*
1 London Bridge Street, London, SE1 9GF

Large Print edition 2018

© 2018 Linda Susan Meier

ISBN: 978-0-263-07382-9

MIX
Paper from
responsible sources
FSC C007454

This book is produced from independently certified
FSC™ paper to ensure responsible forest management.
For more information visit www.harpercollins.co.uk/green.

Printed and bound in Great Britain
by CPI Group (UK) Ltd, Croydon, CR0 4YY

To my mum, an avid reader,
who taught me to love every story.

CHAPTER ONE

RICCARDO OCHOA DROVE under the portico of the Midnight Sins Hotel on the Las Vegas strip. He got out of his rental—a black Mercedes convertible with white leather interior—and tossed the keys to the valet.

"Don't take it too far," he told the twentysomething kid dressed in neat-as-a-pin trousers and a white shirt. "I don't intend to be long."

He turned to enter the hotel and almost ran in to a gaggle of giggling women. "Good afternoon, ladies."

They stopped. Wide-eyed and no longer giggling, the women stared at him.

He hadn't been living in New York City for years without recognizing that his Spanish accent intrigued American women. As did his dark hair, dark eyes and the fact that he worked out five days a week. To them, he was exotic.

The woman wearing a strapless red velvet dress

took a step closer. Her brown hair had been pulled into curls on top of her head. Her green eyes were sultry, seductive. "Are you going inside?"

He smiled at her. "As a matter of fact, I am."

"Maybe I should ditch my friends and join you?"

If he hadn't been there on business, he probably would have taken her up on her offer for a few hours of drinking and gambling. Just some fun. That might have morphed into a night of romance, but that was it. Not because he didn't believe in relationships. He'd seen them work. His cousins Mitch and Alonzo had married beautiful women and were as happy as two guys could be.

But some men weren't built for that kind of life. Riccardo had tried it and had had his heart ripped out of his chest and stomped on—publicly—when his fiancée left him two days before their wedding to reunite with her ex. Gowns had been bought. Tuxes had hung in closets. White-linen-covered tables had lined the rolling lawn of Northern Spain's Ochoa Vineyards, and she'd walked out without a backward glance.

Humiliation had caused him to swear off relationships, but over the next few years, he'd grown to appreciate the benefits of being single. Not to mention rich. When a man had money, the world was at his fingertips. Though it was his cousin Mitch who had started their company, Ochoa Online, Riccardo took the income Mitch's websites generated, invested it and made them millionaires, on the fast track to become billionaires. He more than earned his keep.

Which was why he was in Vegas. With the creative genius behind Ochoa Online away on an extended honeymoon, and one of Mitch's best customers having trouble with his daughter, Riccardo had to shift from moneyman to client problem solver.

"Sorry." He took the hand of the woman in red velvet and caught her gaze before kissing her knuckles. "I'm here on business."

She swallowed. "Maybe when your business is done?"

"I'm picking somebody up and driving us both back to the airport." Morgan Monroe, daughter of Colonel Monroe, owner of Monroe Wines, had run from her wedding. The Colonel wanted her home not just to explain, but for damage control. "I'll be here two hours, tops." He released her hand. "Maybe we'll be lucky enough to meet on my next trip."

"Maybe."

He nodded at her and her friends. "Goodbye, ladies."

The little group said, "Goodbye," and he walked toward the hotel door, which opened automatically. The sleek, modern lobby welcomed him.

He stopped at the concierge. "I'm looking for Morgan Monroe." Unlike his ex, Cicely, who'd at least given him two days' warning, Morgan Monroe had walked halfway down the aisle before she'd turned and run. Her dad had asked his staff to monitor her credit cards and the next day this hotel had popped up. "I'm told she's a guest here."

The fiftysomething gentleman didn't even glance at his computer. "I'm sorry, sir. We don't give away guest information."

"I'm only asking because her father, *Colonel Monroe*," Riccardo said, deliberately dropping the name of her famous father, "sent me."

The man's face whitened. "Her dad is Colonel Monroe?"

Riccardo unobtrusively slid his hand into his

trouser pocket to get a one-hundred-dollar bill. "The same."

"I love his wine."

"Everybody loves his wine." He eased the bill across the polished counter. "He just wants me to make sure she's okay." And bring her home. But the concierge didn't need to know that.

The man casually took the bill off the counter and stuffed it into his pocket. "It's against policy to give you her room number, but friend to friend," he said, motioning for Riccardo to lean closer, "I can tell you I saw her going into the casino about an hour ago. I also happen to know she plays penny slots and loves margaritas. She's been in the same spot in the far right-hand corner every afternoon since she got here."

Though Riccardo groaned internally at the thought of getting a drunk woman into his car and onto a plane, he smiled appreciatively at the concierge. "Thank you."

He turned away from the serene lobby and faced the casino. Twenty steps took him down a ramp, out of the quiet and into a cacophony of noise. Bells and whistles from slots mixed with cheering at the gaming tables and blended with keno numbers. He inhaled deeply. He loved a good casino.

But he didn't even pause at the rows of slot machines or the game tables, where an elderly gentleman appeared to be hot at blackjack. He made his way through the jumble of people and paraphernalia to the penny slots in the far right-hand corner.

No one was there.

He looked to the left, then the right. He'd walked so far back the noise of the casino was only a dull hum behind him. The vacant slots around him were also silent.

Confusion rumbled through him. Though Monday afternoons typically weren't as busy as weekend afternoons, the entire corner was weirdly quiet.

"I'm telling you. When you have as little money as you guys have, you can't play the stock market."

Riccardo's head snapped up.

"But my cousin Arnie netted a bundle playing the market!"

"Because of a lucky guess." The woman talking sighed heavily. "Look, your primary goal should be to make money without losing any of your initial investment."

Curious, Riccardo followed the sounds of the conversation. He walked down the row and turned right, then stopped. Two cocktail waitresses, an old guy in shorts and a Hawaiian shirt, a young guy in a hoodie and two women leaned against the corner machine as a slim blonde in jeans and gray canvas tennis shoes counseled them.

"You can't guarantee you'll keep your initial investment buying individual stocks. Mutual funds mitigate the risk."

One of the waitresses saw Riccardo and nudged her head in his direction. The woman doling out investment advice turned, and Riccardo's mouth fell open.

He knew it was stupid to think Morgan Monroe would still be in the wedding gown she'd had on when she bolted from St. Genevieve church on Saturday, but he also hadn't expected to see Colonel Monroe's high-society daughter in blue jeans and canvas tennis shoes. Her long blond hair hung past her shoulders in tangled disarray. Her enormous blue eyes speared him from behind the lenses of oversize tortoiseshell glasses.

"Get lost, buddy."

He also hadn't expected her to snipe at him. Oh, he'd been sure there'd be a little resistance to his putting her on a plane and taking her back to Lake Justice, home of her father's enormous wine empire. But everything he'd read about Morgan portrayed her as a demure, sweet woman who loved charity work and took in stray cats.

Either the press had absolutely got her wrong, her dad had a really good PR machine, or Morgan Monroe had snapped.

Considering she'd gotten halfway down the aisle at her eight-hundred-person wedding and then turned and run, he was guessing she'd snapped.

He suddenly wondered if that's what had happened with Cicely. If she'd snapped when she'd called off their wedding—

His heart chugged to a stop. He hadn't thought about Cicely in years and today he couldn't stop thinking about her, comparing his situation to Morgan Monroe's. He didn't like remembering the humiliation any more than he liked being reminded that it was his own damn fault. Arrogance had made him believe he could make her love him, though she'd told him time and again that she had an ex she couldn't forget. And pride sure as hell went before his fall.

So, what was he doing getting involved with another runaway bride? Was he nuts?

No. He was helping a client. Plus, the situations were totally different. Cicely had been his fiancée. Morgan was the daughter of the owner of the biggest vineyard on Mitch's wine website. Riccardo did not intend to get *involved* with her beyond taking her home to her dad. This wasn't just a favor for their best client. It was the only way to keep the beloved, world-renowned Colonel from dumping them to start his own wine website and becoming their competition.

Morgan Monroe barely held back a sigh of annoyance with the guy staring at her. He was good-looking, obviously rich—if his tailored white shirt and Italian leather loafers were any indicator—and clearly confused, just standing there as if he had no idea what to do.

Guessing he had been startled to find someone doling out investment advice by the penny slots, she gave him the benefit of the doubt, and said, "There's a sea of machines behind you. You can

play any one you want. And if you go at least a
row away, you won't even hear us."

The surprise on his face was replaced by chagrin. "Holding a little stock seminar, are you?"

His voice wasn't exactly condescending. She
really couldn't tell what it was. But if he thought
she would let him insult these people who needed
her help, he was mistaken.

"If I were, it would be none of your business."

The chagrin became a wince. "That's not true.
I'm actually looking for you... Morgan."

Her chest squeezed. She'd expected her dad
to come searching for her. But this guy didn't
look like a private investigator. She glanced at
the black trousers and fitted shirt again. Open at
the throat, the white shirt revealed tan skin, as if
he summered in the Mediterranean. With his accent, he probably did.

"*You're* a PI?"

"No. I'm a friend of your father."

That was infinitely worse. A PI she could handle. A friend of her dad's? That would take some
finesse.

She turned to her group. "I'm sorry, guys. I'm
going to need a few minutes. Just stay here. I'll

be right back." She walked toward her dad's minion, pointing at the raised circular bar in the middle of the room. "There's a table open up there."

Heading for the bar, she assumed the guy would follow her. She used the two minutes of skirting people, slot machines and gaming tables to remind herself she was twenty-five, educated and in desperate need of some time alone. No matter how this guy approached this, she could say, "Tell my dad I love him and I'm sorry he spent a lot of money on the wedding...but I needed some air."

No. She couldn't tell a perfect stranger she needed some air. That was stupid. Her dad would roar with fury if she sent this admittedly handsome guy back to him without something concrete.

She reached to pull out her chair, but Handsome Spanish Guy beat her to it.

Giving her a polite smile, he said, "My nanna would shoot me if I let a woman get her own chair."

She sat. "Your nanna?"

"My grandmother." He sat across from her. "She lives in Spain. Very much old-school. She likes men with manners."

So did Morgan. And, wow, she loved this guy's voice. Smooth and sexy with just enough accent to make him interesting.

But he was here because her dad had sent him. She shouldn't be noticing that he was attractive. Plus, she'd just walked out on her own wedding. After leaving one guy at the altar two days ago, she was not in the market for another. No matter how gorgeous.

She cleared her throat. "Okay. My dad sent you to find me—"

"I didn't have to find you. He knows where you are. He wants me to bring you home."

She gaped at him. "He knows where I am?"

"Did you think I just strolled into this hotel on a lucky guess?"

"No." As a former secretary of state and a current high-profile business owner, her dad had more money than God and resources to do things Morgan was only beginning to understand. She didn't need to know how her dad had found her. The point was, he had.

She pulled in a breath and released it slowly enough to get her thoughts together. "Okay, Marco Polo, here's the deal. The next two weeks had been blocked off for a honeymoon. My dad has an event in Stockholm two days after that, so I have to be home before he leaves. But that also means I don't have to be anywhere for another twelve days." She planted her backside a little more firmly on the chair. "I'm not going anywhere."

"Yes, you are. You left your dad with eight hundred confused guests filling the bed-and-breakfasts in town, waiting to see if you're okay, not to mention one very disoriented fiancé. You're not dodging the damage control."

She rose from her seat. "I didn't want the eight hundred guests. Charles did. I didn't want the wedding reception at the vineyard. That was my dad's handiwork. I picked out the dress and my bouquet." Her eyes unexpectedly filled with tears and the emotions that had hit her as she walked down the aisle spiraled through her again. The betrayal. The sense of stupidity for trusting Charles. The sense of stupidity for being so trusting—period.

She very quickly said, "If you'll excuse me," turned and headed back to her cluster of new friends, not willing to let this stranger see her cry.

Damn it. She'd thought she'd worked through all this in the plane.

She raised her chin. She *had* dealt with all this on the commuter flight to JFK, while shopping for clothes to change into in the big airport and on the flight to Vegas. That reaction to talking about her wedding was simply a release of stress. She was not unhappy that she'd left Charles. She seriously didn't care that her dad's life had been inconvenienced. She'd told them and told them and told them that she wanted a small wedding. No one listened, and eventually she'd let it drop. Because that's what she'd done since she was twelve, when her mom had died and she suddenly became lady of the house.

Not old enough to really know what to do, she'd taken her father's advice on everything. That had become such a habit she didn't even realize she'd let him pick the man she'd marry. For as much as her dad had nudged her in Charles's direction with frequent dinners at their home and trips to London, Ireland and Monaco that coincided with trips Charles was taking, her dad had also groomed Charles to be his son-in-law.

They'd seemed like the ultimate power couple

until Charles's best man mentioned that fact at the rehearsal-dinner toast. Even he'd seen how Charles had been groomed and all Morgan had to do was wait until her father's creation was finished to have the perfect man to add to their two-person family.

The crowd had laughed, but her chest had pressed inward, squeezing all the air from her lungs. His toast, no matter how lighthearted, had a ring of truth to it. No. More like a gong of truth. A whole Mormon Tabernacle Choir of truth.

And Charles's response when she'd confronted him after the dinner? He'd needed her dad's help. If marrying her was the price, he'd pay it.

When she'd gasped, he'd said he didn't mean that the way it sounded. He loved her. She was beautiful. Wonderful. A woman so perfect she was more like a reward, not a price. He was sorry his explanation had come out all wrong.

For the hours that had passed between the toast and her trip down the aisle, she'd believed that.

But there was something about walking toward her destiny, dressed in all white, looking sweet and innocent while perpetuating something that felt very much like fraud, that caused her feet to stop, her heart to break. Her dad had controlled everything in her life, from where she'd gone to school to how she dressed and who she'd invite to their gatherings. The man she spent the rest of her life with would be her choice.

"You okay?" Mary, the lead waitress for the afternoon shift, studied her as she walked back to her little investment group beside the last row of slots.

She sucked in a breath and smiled. "I'm fine." She *was* fine. Though Charles was history, she wasn't writing off her dad completely. This was a hiccup in their relationship. A time for her to take a breath, sort out what she wanted, maybe come up with some new rules for how she and her dad would relate. Then she would go back to Lake Justice. Then they would talk.

And no gorgeous Spaniard with a sexy voice was taking her back before she was ready.

CHAPTER TWO

RICCARDO STAYED AT the two-person table in the bar. From the raised vantage point, he could see Morgan as she counseled her little band of friends. She was a lot stronger than he'd imagined. He didn't want to admire her for it. It was his job to bring her home. But he had to admit to a twinge of respect that she could hold her own. Which was good. He didn't want to feel like he was riding roughshod over her by forcing her onto the plane. He wanted her to see the error of her ways and go home voluntarily to do her duty to her ex. That was more than Cicely had done for him.

He winced. Seriously. He had to stop comparing the two. At least Cicely had talked to him two days before their wedding and been honest. Morgan had just run. She'd embarrassed her groom. Embarrassed her dad. Shocked her guests. And now she wanted to give stock seminars?

Okay. That did speak to her state of mind. Ignoring something wasn't always a sign of indifference. Maybe she wasn't ready to handle it yet.

Who was he? Doctor Phil? It was not his job to fix her, just to get her home.

Of course, it wouldn't hurt to keep her mental state in mind as he guided her to see the error of her ways and agree to come back home with him.

That's what Mitch would do. And Mitch was their people person.

When the small group broke up, Riccardo glanced at his watch. Twenty minutes had gone by. Their flight left in an hour and a half. But it was a short ride to the airport. Of course, he should probably add packing time in there. He might not have luggage, but she did.

Or maybe not.

She'd run from the ceremony, jumped into her car and had gotten to Lake Justice's small municipal airport in a matter of minutes. She'd caught the commuter flight that just happened to be leaving for JFK International, and that's why they'd lost her. The plane had taken off as her dad's people were pulling in to the small airport parking lot.

He could imagine her arriving at Kennedy in her gown, stopping at the first shop she saw and buying some jeans, T-shirts and those superspiffy canvas tennis shoes.

He laughed into his beer before he finished it in one long swallow. He seriously doubted she would want to take home any of the clothes she'd bought if they were anything like what she was wearing now. But he would be more sensitive, more Mitch-like, when he approached her this time.

Except she'd better not call him Marco Polo again. Marco Polo wasn't even Spanish.

The group dispersed. Morgan took a seat at the last slot machine. She pulled her comp card out of her jeans pocket, inserted it into the poker machine and started playing.

Riccardo rose, tossed a few bills on the bar table and ambled over to her. He sat on the seat of the empty machine beside hers. "So… Our flight leaves in an hour and a half. I know it's a short ride to the airport, but we do have to go through security."

"*Your* flight leaves in an hour and a half."

"*Our* flight. You're coming with me. You're too

nice of a woman to leave your groom upset and wondering what the hell happened."

"I seriously doubt Charles is upset. We'd had a disagreement the night before. He thought he'd talked me out of being angry. But I'd never been angry. I was hurt. Which means, once again, he didn't hear what I was saying. Only what he wanted to hear. When I get home, he'll have a ten-point plan for how we can fix things. And he doesn't even really know what's wrong. I have twelve days until I have to be back and I'm taking them."

He wanted to argue, but saw her point. Something had caused her to run from her own wedding. But it sounded like Charles didn't care to talk it through. All he wanted was to fix things. That wasn't very romantic. Or sensitive. Or even nice.

He hated having to drag her back to that, but all he had was her version of things. He knew what it was like to be the brokenhearted groom, totally confused—

And, once again, he was thinking about his own situation, which was entirely different and completely irrelevant. If he was going to take Morgan

Monroe home, perhaps he would have to get her to talk about whatever it was that had hurt *her* and caused *her* to bolt, and stop thinking about Cicely. Then Morgan would feel better about returning to Lake Justice, and Mitch wouldn't come home from his honeymoon to find his biggest client gone—and becoming their competition.

He leaned his elbow on the poker machine and studied her. When he'd first seen her, she'd seemed out of place. But really, in her jeans and T-shirt, with her long hair casual, she looked like the average slot player on a Monday afternoon.

He nodded at her machine. "You like poker?"

She peeked over at him, her blue eyes a pretty contrast to the tortoiseshell glasses. "To be honest, I'm just learning to play."

"That would explain why you threw away the chance for a straight flush."

"Odds are I'm not going to get it."

He bobbed his head in a sort of agreement. "Yeah, but when the machine gives you four cards in a row in the same suit and you have two open ends, your odds go up."

"Odds are odds."

"What are you? An accountant?"

She glanced over at him. "Yes."

He remembered the little stock seminar and felt like an idiot for not realizing that. He knew she was educated but he'd never thought a society girl would pick such a practical major. Her dad only talked about her charities. He'd made her sound like a sort of helpless Southern belle though they lived in upstate New York.

"You're like a CPA?"

"I *am* a CPA."

Her machine gurgled the music of a lost game and she hit a few buttons to make her bets and start the next game. Cards appeared on the screen. She threw away two twos.

His eyes narrowed. "What are you doing?"

"Two twos don't pay out."

"No. But three of a kind does. So does two pair. Starting off with two twos you have a good chance of getting another two or another pair and both of those hands pay."

"Chump change."

He laughed. "What?"

"I want to win. I don't just want to keep playing."

That was a weird strategy if ever he'd heard

one. And he'd certainly heard his share in Monaco. "Who taught you that?"

"The guy who was sitting beside me on Sunday night."

"He was a professional gambler?"

"No. He manages a couple fast-food restaurants."

"And you thought this made him a genius poker player?"

She tossed her hands in the air. "Hell if I know."

He scooted over to get closer to her. He'd take this opportunity to become her friend and eventually she'd spill the story. He could sympathize and in a few minutes they'd be in his rental, heading for the airport.

"Okay, look." He pointed at the ranking of hands. "See this list here? This is what pays out and how many points."

"I know that."

"If you have a pattern that you use all the time, the machine will become accustomed to it and use that against you."

Her pale blue eyes narrowed.

"If you only go for what seems like a sure thing, it will set you up so that you keep getting those opportunities, then never give you the cards you need to make the hands, so that you lose all your money."

"Oh." She thought about that a second. "I should shake it up? Not play the same way all the time."

"Exactly. But on another trip." Now that they were friends, or at least friendly, they could talk about her wedding in the car. "Right now, we need to get you home."

She looked over at him. "We have to leave this very second? What's a few more hands going to hurt? I just want to try out what you told me."

He'd expected a bit of a protest. Maybe an argument. But getting her to think about her fiancé must have caused it to sink in that she had to take responsibility for what she'd done. She hadn't even blinked when he mentioned leaving.

He caught her gaze and saw a muddle of emotions in her blue eyes. Sincerity? Regret? Or maybe fear? She wasn't exactly returning to a celebration.

A twinge of guilt rippled through him for pushing her. The least he could do was teach her some strategies.

"Okay. A few hands."

"And you'll show me what to do?"

"Sure."

He didn't know how it happened, but a couple of hands turned into forty minutes of playing, which put them behind the eight ball. Though she'd seemed to have had a good time and was definitely a quick study, the fun had to end now.

"Okay. That's it now. Time to go."

She hit the button to cash out and got the little slip that told her she had thirty-eight dollars coming.

"Huh."

"What?"

"Thirty-eight dollars." She caught his gaze. "Hardly seems worth it."

"Most people who gamble enjoy the game."

"Really? Because I've seen video poker games that are handheld. Our cook, Martha, has a ton of them. It's how she fritters away time waiting for doctor appointments or bread to rise."

He shrugged. "People enjoy the game."

"Yes, but she doesn't spend money playing. She owns her handheld machines and can *enjoy* anytime she wants."

He sighed.

"If it's all about playing a game, enjoying a game, why not just buy the game? Why involve betting?"

"Are you trying to ruin Vegas for me?"

She laughed. "No. I mean, come on. If playing the game is the attraction and not gambling, why not just use a handheld poker game?"

This time his sigh was eloquent. "Do *not* ruin Vegas for me."

"I'm not ruining it. I'm just pointing out that your argument doesn't hold water."

"You're a stickler for logic." And obviously so was her fiancé. Anybody who'd have a ten-point plan to fix their canceled wedding had to be logical. Was that how they'd ended up together? Two people who were so much the same it seemed inevitable that they get married?

"I *am* a stickler for logic. So sway me. Why do you really come to casinos?"

He looked into her eyes again and saw the quiet remnants of pain, even though she was very good at pretending she was fine. If talking about himself made her comfortable, calm enough that she'd be compliant through their trip, then so be it.

He shrugged. "I come to Vegas for the people, the crowds, the noise, the excitement." He couldn't stop a smile. "You never know who you're going to meet here. You can sit beside a sheikh at a blackjack table and end up a guest at a palace. Or meet the daughter of a rock star and end up backstage at a concert."

"Interesting."

She glanced around. The way her eyes shifted, he could tell she was seeing the place from a new perspective. If only for a few seconds, her sadness lifted.

"It's about people for you."

"Yes." It was one thing to help her get comfortable, quite another to let this conversation derail his plans. He'd be happy to discuss anything she wanted, just not now. He pointed to the exit. "But we'll talk about it on the way to the airport or on the plane."

She slid off her chair. "I have to pack."

"You have five minutes! I'm serious. *Five.* I'll get the car."

She nodded.

He started walking away but turned back. "And, honestly, I have no idea why you'd want these clothes. If I were you, I'd leave them."

She laughed.

A strange sensation invaded his chest. Even in those big glasses, she was incredibly beautiful. Add adorably logical and laughing—

He yanked himself back from the feeling that almost clicked into place. Attraction. He wasn't worried that he'd fall for her. His heart had been sufficiently hardened by Cicely. So the pullback was quick, easy, painless. Especially given that Morgan had also publicly dumped some poor guy.

He headed out to the valet. When the kid returned with his rental car, he gave him a good tip for being speedy. He slid behind the steering wheel and locked his gaze on the door. The first five minutes had already passed, so when a second five minutes ticked off the clock he got nervous. The third five minutes had him slapping the steering wheel. She'd ditched him.

He shoved open his door, apologized to the valet for needing a few more minutes and raced into the lobby, hoping to see her checking out at the registration desk. But the place was quiet.

The concierge slipped away from his station and ambled up to him. "Your friend left."

He spun to face the short, bald man. "What?"

"She checked out, rolled her suitcase through the casino—not the front door—and slipped out of one of the back exits." He cleared his throat. "I probably shouldn't have watched her, but it's kind of hard not to see a beautiful woman rolling an ugly black suitcase through the casino."

Riccardo pressed his fingertips into his forehead. He'd been duped. And in the most obvious, simple way. She'd used up all their time, gotten him to trust her and just walked away.

He was an idiot.

No. He had trusted her.

Hadn't he told himself he should never again trust a pretty girl?

Morgan entered her new room at the hotel right beside Midnight Sins. She felt just a teeny bit bad for deceiving the handsome Spanish guy. Not just because her dad had made him a pawn in a game that didn't have to be a game—she only wanted her twelve days to think about what to say, and how to handle him when she went home—but also because he was interesting. And fun. In a weird way, it was nice having someone so curious about her, even if it he was only asking her questions to figure out how to get her on the plane with him.

She took a shower, fixed her hair and slid into a slinky black dress she'd bought at one of the many shops in Midnight Sins. She wasn't here to have fun, but she didn't intend to sit in her room and mope, either. She'd spent her entire life semi-isheltered. She'd had a path at university. She'd had a path with Charles. And her dad had had too big of a hand in creating those paths. For the next twelve days, she did not want a path. She just wanted to live. Breathe. And eventually figure out an explanation for running that would appease the man who'd spent his life first fighting in wars and then preventing them.

Right now, living meant getting a salad, maybe having a gin and tonic and going to a show.

She grabbed her small beaded evening bag and left her room. Though she'd never been to Vegas before, she'd happily discovered that once she checked in to a hotel, she didn't need to leave for anything. She could sleep there, gamble there, eat there, buy a bathing suit in a shop and sunbathe at the hotel pool. She would be right under Handsome Spanish Guy's nose and he would never find her because he'd have to check hundreds of hotels. And then he'd have to find someone willing to tell him she was a guest.

The odds were absolutely in her favor.

Happy, she took the regular elevator to the first floor then a designated elevator to the rooftop restaurant, where she had a reservation.

The maître d' greeted her effusively and led her to the private table in the corner. With its walls of windows, the restaurant provided a view of Las Vegas that astounded her. She sat, smiled at the maître d' and took her menu. A minute later she gave her drink order to a friendly waiter and he left her alone to decide what she wanted to eat. She should have at least glanced at her food choices, but the view from forty stories up was too captivating. Lights and color twinkled silently below. Beyond the city, the desert was so dark she swore the world ended at the city limits.

The blackness in the window was interrupted by a strip of white. Something shiny winked. She saw the reflection of a hand.

She spun around and there was Handsome Spanish Guy. The man who wanted to take her home.

"Who are you anyway?"

"Riccardo Ochoa." He pointed at the seat across from her. "May I join you?"

She tossed her hands in despair. "No! What part of 'I'm trying to get some peace and quiet' do you not understand?"

"Well, most of it—since *I* come to Vegas to meet people and have fun."

"I came here to rest my brain. I know I have to go home and face all of this but I just want a breather."

He sighed, pulled out the chair opposite her and sat. "You are not going to make this easy for me, are you?"

"Why do you care?" She sighed. "Look. Whatever my dad is paying you, I'll double it."

"He's not paying me. He's a client of my cousin's firm." He made a quick signal to summon the waiter and ordered a Scotch.

When the waiter left, she said, "And my dad threatened to walk if you didn't bring me home."

"Something like that."

"Well, I hate to disappoint you but if you're counting on taking me home to keep him as a client you're going to lose him."

"Well, I hate to disappoint *you*, but I've never

failed on a mission. Never. When I promised to return you to Lake Justice, you were as good as home."

She shook her head. "So arrogant."

He laughed but the humor didn't reach his eyes. "Sweetheart, I'm Spanish. We invented arrogant."

"It must have really hurt your pride that I lost you." She frowned. "How did you find me so quickly?"

His Scotch came with the drink she had ordered. He took a long swallow. "Your credit card."

"*My* credit card?"

"Your dad got you that card when you were at university, right?"

"Yes, but I took it over. I pay the bill."

"He still has the number and his name is on the account. Yesterday, he realized he could log in online. Now, every time you use it, he sees where you are."

She slapped her evening bag on the white linen tablecloth. "Damn it." She'd been so stressed out, she'd completely forgotten that.

"You're not getting away from me." He smiled. "Unless you have another card."

"I don't." She sighed. "Well, I do, but my dad's

staff got me that one, too." She drank her gin and tonic in one long gulp, thinking through her options, which, right at this moment, stunk.

"Sort of a little too attached to Daddy, maybe?"

She rose. "That's actually the point."

No matter what hotel she checked in to, her dad would know her location from the charge record. No matter where she flew, same deal. She could rent a car, but that would be on a card, too, and even if she drove a hundred miles away, every time she stopped for gas her dad would know where she was.

She started toward the restaurant door.

Riccardo jumped up. "Really? We're going to play this game?"

He pulled a few bills from his pocket and tossed them on the table. When he caught up to her at the elevator, he said, "There's nowhere for you to go. You're trapped."

Oh, she knew that better than anybody else.

She cast him a sideways glance. As long as her dad knew where she was, there would be someone coming after her. If this guy failed, her father would just send somebody else.

She'd already fooled Riccardo Ochoa once. She

liked her odds with fooling him again. And she had a plan. She and her mom had spent many a week in Chicago shopping. She could think things through there just as well as in Vegas. She'd never get Riccardo to fly her to Chicago. But after a bit of time together, she might be able to convince him to drive her there. And she had just the way to do it.

"Do you have a rental?"

"Yes. But I'll be getting rid of it at the airport."

She turned, facing him. His gaze rippled from her bare shoulders, past the shimmery sequins of the bodice of her dress to the hem where her skirt stopped midthigh.

The quick look was as intimate as a caress. A light flickered in his dark eyes. She would bet if this guy was interested in her romantically, there wouldn't be a dull moment. Their summer vacation wouldn't be a trip to Europe to meet with clients. He'd take her somewhere hot and steamy—

She stepped back, away from him. The last thing she wanted was a man attracted to her when she hadn't properly dealt with Charles. But she also needed this guy. She had to keep their relationship platonic.

"I don't want to fly. I don't want to be in Lake Justice any sooner than I have to be. Drive me—" She felt a prick of conscience, but desperation overwhelmed it. She was twenty-five. *Twenty-five.* And her dad was theoretically kidnapping her. This was her only move. "Instead of forcing me to fly, and I'll have a few days to think things through, while my dad calms down." She caught the gaze of his very suspicious black eyes and smiled prettily, innocently. "I just want a couple of days of peace and quiet. A car ride will give me that as well as give you something to tell my dad about why it's taking you so long to get me back."

Those dark eyes studied her. "You won't run?"

"No."

"You won't sneak out of a hotel room in the middle of the night?"

"You'll have the only keys to the car."

He still deliberated.

She stood quietly, but confidently. She didn't intend to sneak out, steal the car, or ditch him. True, she wanted him to take her to Chicago to extend their trip for an additional few days, but she'd cross that bridge when they came to it.

"Okay."

"Good. Just let me get my bags."

He laughed heartily. "Right. This time I'm coming with you."

CHAPTER THREE

THEY STEPPED OVER the threshold of her hotel room and Morgan immediately ducked into the bathroom. Riccardo ambled into the small room, but not far. He wasn't letting her get much more than an arm's distance away from him until they were at her daddy's vineyard.

His conscience grumbled a protest. When he'd accepted this assignment, he'd done it out of desperation, to protect everything he and Mitch had built. He hadn't thought much about the situation beyond the fact that Morgan had dumped her fiancé and she needed to come home and explain herself. Then she'd told him a bit about her fiancé and he'd felt sorry for her.

Then she'd duped him and now he was super suspicious of her.

But he couldn't stop thinking about her ex's ten-point plan and the sadness he'd heard in her voice. If he were to guess, he'd say she genuinely believed her fiancé hadn't loved her.

She stepped out of the bathroom wearing jeans, a tank top and the gray canvas tennis shoes. The curls had been combed out of her long blond hair and she'd pulled it into a ponytail. Her glasses were gone and he suspected she'd put in contacts. She looked innocently beautiful. So beautiful that he could probably disabuse her of the notion that her fiancé hadn't loved her. There wasn't a man on the planet who wouldn't fall for that face.

"You may not like my clothing choices but they are going to come in handy driving across the country."

He couldn't argue that. Or the fact that she was beginning to look really cute in jeans. Not quite hot. More like sweet and cuddly.

Thank goodness. Sweet he could resist. Hot? The way she'd looked in that form-fitting black dress? That was his wheelhouse. Instinct had almost taken over and he'd wanted to touch her, to smooth his hands along the lovely curve of her waist. But he hadn't because he was smart. And now she was dressed like a good girl, not the kind of woman a man played with. She was perfectly safe.

So was he.

In the hall outside her room, he took the handle of the cheap black suitcase that she'd probably bought at the worst shop she could find in the airport on her way here.

"I'll get this."

She smiled sweetly. "Thanks."

He wanted to trust that she really was this compliant, that the promise of several days on the road to calm her nerves had satisfied her. But his pride still stung from the way she'd ditched him at Midnight Sins.

They rode down the elevator and she used her credit card to check out. Then she motioned for him to follow her to an ATM. She withdrew cash three times, getting as much money as she could before the bank shut her off.

"Planning your escape?"

"No. Paying for my own food and hotel."

"You could use the credit card for that. Your dad's going to know where you are. Might as well just roll with it."

She said nothing, simply walked out the front

door, her head high, as if it took great effort to preserve her pride, and his damn conscience nudged him again.

He scrambled after her. "It's not like I'm kidnapping you."

"If you were, I could at least call the police. As it is, with my dad behind your taking me away, you're more like a jailer."

"I'm not a jailer."

"Sure you are. You're keeping me from going where I want to go."

They strode the short distance back to Midnight Sins and he tossed his car keys to the valet, who rolled his eyes as he raced away to get Riccardo's rental.

"I don't know what he has to complain about. He gets a tip every time he takes or brings back my car."

She laughed.

His spirits rose a little. If she could laugh, then he shouldn't feel too bad. Because she was right. With the way all this was going down, he *was* her jailer. Or her guard. Which meant she probably felt like a prisoner.

The valet returned and handed the keys to Riccardo, who gave him a tip way beyond what he deserved.

He stowed Morgan's suitcase in the trunk before getting behind the wheel. "I just realized that I don't have anything to wear for five days on the road," he said. "I'd planned on flying to Vegas and back to Lake Justice in the same day."

"I'm sure we'll pass a discount store along the way."

"Discount store?" He glanced over at her as he started the car. He didn't like being judgmental, but he was just about positive she'd never seen the inside of a big-box store.

But, of course, *she* wasn't going to shop there, she was sending him there.

Because she had a low opinion of him?

Probably.

He shouldn't care. No matter what she thought, she wasn't a prisoner. And he was more like the accountability police than a jailer. He was taking her back to deal with the fallout from her canceled wedding so that cleaning up the mess didn't default to her dad or her undoubtedly shell-shocked fiancé. He was doing a good thing, and on some level, she had to agree or she wouldn't be on the seat beside his.

He pulled the gearshift into Drive and eased off the hotel property into the traffic of the Vegas strip. In the time that had passed since his arrival, they'd transitioned from afternoon to evening. Hotel fountains now spewed water through glorious colored lights. Neon signs began to glow.

Realizing he had no clue where he was going, he took his phone out of his pocket, set it on the dashboard and said, "Directions to Lake Justice, New York."

After a few seconds, his GPS told him to turn around. He glanced at the green road sign up ahead and sighed. "We're going the wrong way."

Morgan didn't reply.

The GPS took him to the first street where he could make a right. He turned around and headed out to the strip again, except in the opposite direction.

"Okay. Now, we're on our way."

She said nothing.

Fine. They could spend the next four or five days in total silence and he'd be happy. She'd probably be happy, too. She'd said she wanted time to think things through. Well, he would give it to her. Jailers or guards or even accountability police didn't try to make friends with prisoners. They just got them to their destinations.

He refused to feel guilty.

Refused.

Except she'd said her fiancé didn't listen to her. The idiot had thought she was angry, when she was hurt. Hurt enough to run out on a wedding with eight hundred guests.

Curiosity begged him to ask her about it. Especially since this was nothing like his own past. His fiancée had gone back to the love of her life. Morgan had run to nothing. No one.

The fact that she was quiet made him feel like scum. Even more than when she called him her jailer.

It didn't take long until they were on the highway, headed northeast to pick up the roads that would take them east. When they left the lights of Las Vegas, the world became eerily dark. Time passed. Riccardo wasn't sure how much because he'd been so concerned with getting Morgan into the car that he hadn't checked his watch to see when they'd started out.

He shifted on his seat, uncomfortably aware that he'd awoken at six o'clock that morning in the eastern time zone. And it was now after ten at night, mountain time. Midnight in New York. No wonder his eyelids were scratchy. And he couldn't even remember the last time he'd eaten.

"Want to stop to find someplace to stay for the night and get dinner?"

"Sure."

Her reply wasn't exactly perky or happy, but she didn't sound sad anymore, either. Ten minutes later, the road signs for a town began to appear, including one that named the available hotels and restaurants. He took the exit and drove to the first hotel.

With Morgan standing beside him, he booked a room for each of them using his own credit card. When he handed her key to her, she gave him the cash to cover her room. Then she took the handle of her suitcase and headed for the elevator.

"Don't you want dinner?"

She stopped and faced him. "I'll eat breakfast."

She turned toward the elevator again, got in and disappeared behind the closing door.

He almost cursed. But not quite. She might not

be angry with *him* but upset with the situation. And the situation was her doing, her problem. Not his. It was not his fault she had no support system. He'd rescued one damsel in distress—Cicely, who had been heartbroken over losing the love of her life—and that had ended in *him* being humiliated. He had learned this lesson and refused to fall into the same trap. He was a driver—he'd settled on that instead of jailer—not a knight in shining armor.

Besides, he needed something to eat. He didn't even have a suitcase to drop off in his room. He could go now.

He walked to the sliding glass door of the popular chain hotel. It opened automatically and he turned to the right. A twenty-four-hour, diner-type restaurant was within walking distance. He strolled over, found a booth and ordered a burger and fries.

When his food arrived, his stomach danced. But when he picked up the hamburger and opened his mouth to take the first delicious bite, he remembered that Morgan had been in a restaurant, menu in front of her, when he'd barged in on her and reminded her that he'd always be able to find her because of her credit card. She'd been in that restaurant because she was hungry. No matter what she'd just said.

He sighed, put the burger back on his plate and hailed the waitress again.

"Is something wrong?"

He smiled. "Actually, it looks and smells delicious but I left my friend back at the hotel. Could I get a burger and fries to go for her?" The waitress nodded but before she turned away, he lifted his plate. "And could you put this in a to-go container, too?"

She took his plate. "I'll be glad to."

Twenty minutes later, he arrived back at the hotel with a bag containing two orders of fries and two burgers. Remembering her room number, he pushed the elevator button for her floor and inhaled deeply as the little car climbed. When the bell chimed, he stepped out and walked down the hall.

He hesitated at her door but only for a second. His nanna would shoot him for letting anyone go hungry, especially a woman in his custody.

He knocked twice and waited. After a few seconds, her door opened as far as the chain lock would allow.

"Checking up on me, Mr. Jailer?"

"No." He displayed the bag of food. "I bought you a hamburger."

"Leave it outside my door. I'll get it."

"Come on. Let me in. I'm sorry for my part in this but I made a promise and I keep my promises. If you're angry, it's because you don't like the idea of going back and facing the music."

She closed the door, undid the chain lock and opened it again. "No. I'm angry because I honest-to-God thought I'd get almost two weeks to think all this through before I had to go home and settle things with my dad and Charles." She motioned him over to the small table at the back of the room. "I should have laughed at the best man's dumb wedding toast, but what he'd said was true. My dad *had* groomed Charles to be his son-in-law and I'd fallen in line like a fluffy sheep. I would like a few days to consider all sides of the argument I'm about to have, so I'll know what to say and I can win."

His curiosity about how she hadn't seen what was going on and had been a sheep almost overwhelmed him. But if he asked for specifics he'd become involved and he didn't want to be involved. Rescuing Cicely had been enough.

He pulled the containers out of the bag and set them on the table. "You can think the entire drive." She didn't reply, but he noticed she also didn't say no to the food. "The orders are the same. Bacon burgers and fries."

She smiled stupidly. "I haven't had a burger in years." She peeked over at him. "Not since college."

"Really?"

"There's a lot of fat in beef."

"I know. I love it."

She shook her head then sat on one of the two chairs at the table. "At least I don't have to worry about fitting into a gown."

Taking his cue from her, he sat on the chair across from her. "There is that."

She bit into the hamburger and groaned in ecstasy. "That's so freaking good."

He laughed.

She tried a fry and her eyes closed as she savored it. "I can't eat like this the whole trip. We have to have a salad now and again."

"Noted." He also noted she hadn't called him a jailer again and she was making small talk. He bit into his burger and his stomach sighed with relief. He ate three bites and four fries before he realized she'd gone silent again.

She did have things to work out before she talked to her dad. But his curiosity rose again. Plus, he didn't want her to be sad for five long days. Surely, he could hear the story without wanting to jump in and fix things for her.

"What did your fiancé's best man say in the toast that made you feel like a sheep?"

She shrugged. "That my dad had groomed Charles to be his *son-in-law*. Not even my husband. *His* son-in-law." She shook her head as if she could shake away the anger. "But it wasn't all about the toast. The toast merely confirmed odd, disjointed thoughts I'd been having for a few months before the wedding. My first doubts appeared while we were planning. I realized that Charles insisted on his own way a lot."

"Were you one of those brides who'd planned her wedding when she was six and got mad when he asked for a few changes?"

"No. It was more that he had this grand, elegant

event planned, and since I was sort of clueless about what I wanted, I went along."

"Makes sense."

For the first time in hours she held his gaze. The sadness was gone from her pretty blue eyes, but not the confusion.

"Yes. At the time, it did."

"But eventually it didn't?"

"No, eventually I saw that he got his own way a lot. That he always told me what we'd be doing. Everything from vacations to whose Christmas parties we'd attend."

"Ah."

"Then I noticed that if I tried to get something my way, he'd bulldoze me." She suddenly closed the lid on her container of food, which was still half-uneaten, and bounced out of her seat. "You know what? That's enough about me and my almost wedding to Charles." She tossed her container in a wastebasket under the small, wooden desk and turned to him with a smile. "I'm tired and I'm talking about things I haven't even worked through."

He understood why her realizations infuriated her enough that she was done talking. Cicely had been all about getting her own way about their wedding, too, and he'd wanted so much to make her happy that he always fell in line.

"I knew somebody like that. We were engaged."

"What happened?"

"She called off the wedding."

She grimaced. "Like me?"

"No. She called it off a few days before so we had a chance to cancel things like flowers and the caterer."

"I'm sorry."

"Hey, I didn't tell you that to make you feel worse. I wanted you to understand that I've dealt with someone who was selfish, too. Cicely didn't let me have a say in our wedding and though she didn't exactly bulldoze, she did have a knack for always getting her own way."

Morgan laughed.

He smiled. "I'm glad you're feeling better."

Her head tilted and her eyes met his. "I don't feel better. I may never feel better. I was suffocating in that dress, walking down the aisle. Turning and running was like saving myself...like a survival instinct." She drew in a breath and huffed it out again. "But I upset people. And I'm not used to that. I'm not used to putting myself first at the expense of others. When I turned and ran, I lost the girl who would never in a million years hurt another person. So, no. I don't feel better. I may never feel better again."

The next morning, he brought breakfast sandwiches to her room. Morgan suspected that was to keep her moving, but he need not have worried. She didn't intend to slow him down. She wanted him to trust her again. When they reached the point in the highway when one simple turn would take them to Chicago, she wanted him to be willing to take it.

"Can I help with your suitcase?"

A week ago, she wouldn't have minded a man being deferential to her. Now? She just wanted to do things herself. To *be* herself. But she wouldn't argue something so stupid and risk alienating him. She let him wheel her bag out to the parking lot.

When they had settled in the car, she pointed up the road. "I see a few stores along there. Do you want to drive over and get a pair of jeans? Maybe a clean shirt or two?"

He laughed. "Do I smell bad? Or are you pro-longing the trip?"

"Neither." She pulled in a breath. There was no time like the present to start the campaign to get him on her side. "As I told you last night, I'm normally a very considerate person. Now that the shock is wearing off, part of the real me must be coming back."

He glanced over. "I get that."

"Do you?"

"Yeah, I thought about what you'd said about how you felt when you bolted, and I realized there probably isn't a person in the world who doesn't understand the feeling of suffocating when you're with someone who always has to have their own way."

Though he didn't know that her dad was really the one suffocating her, she smiled. "Thank you."

The conversation died as he drove them to one of the big-box stores. As they got out of the convertible and headed for the door, she realized she was okay in her jeans and canvas tennis shoes, but in his expensive white shirt and black trousers he looked like he'd just stepped off the Las

Vegas strip—at one of the better hotels. People were going to stare.

The automatic doors opened as they approached. When they walked inside, he got a cart.

She frowned at him. "What are you doing?"

"I need clothes for three or four days." He nodded at his shiny handmade Italian loafers. "I'm not wearing these anymore. I want tennis shoes. Even with two of us to carry things, there'll be too much for us to tote around."

"I'm not talking about the clothes. What are you doing being so familiar with a shopping cart at a retail store?"

He laughed. "I came to this country a few years ago. And I've been exploring ever since. I don't shop at stores like this often but I've investigated them."

It was a real struggle not to laugh, then she wondered why. If she moved to Spain, she'd probably investigate things, too. At least she hoped she would. Lately, she was beginning to realize she didn't know herself at all. Oh, she knew she was kind, a decent human being. But she'd taken a job at her dad's vineyard that wasn't even remotely challenging. She'd let it blow by her that her dad had thrown her and Charles together. And she'd been complacent with Charles. Where was the little girl who'd wanted her life to be an adventure?

She didn't even have to wait for the answer to pop into her head. That little girl had grown up and realized she had only one parent and if she displeased him she'd be all alone.

That was really the bottom line to her battle. Her dad was her only family. She loved him and didn't want to fight or argue. But she was an adult now, not a little girl, and she couldn't let him go on telling her what to do and how to do it. She had to take her life back.

Still, her dad was a brilliant, powerful man, accustomed to getting his own way. Could she make him see he was suffocating her? And if she did, would he stop? *Could* he stop?

Or was the real solution to her problem to leave? Permanently. Pack her bags. Get an apartment. And never see him again.

The thought shot pain through her.

That's why she needed the few days. To adjust to the fact that the conversation she needed to have with her dad just might be their last.

* * *

Riccardo recognized that his familiarity with the store totally puzzled Morgan, but within minutes he was preoccupied with getting himself enough clothes for what would probably be another four days on the road.

They returned to the rental car, drove back to the highway and were on the road for six hours before they stopped to get a late lunch. They drove and drove and drove until afternoon became evening and evening became night and—honestly—his backside hurt.

"I think we should stop for the night."

She shrugged. "Okay."

"I thought I'd shower and put on clean clothes, then we could get something to eat."

"Sure."

Her one-word answer didn't annoy him. It simply made him feel funny. After almost two days together, hearing bits and pieces of some of the most emotional, wrenching parts of her life, it seemed weird that she was back to behaving as if they were strangers. It was good that she was no longer calling him her jailer, but he knew there was something she wasn't telling him. He'd thought through her scenario—her dad grooming her fiancé and her fiancé being clueless—and nothing about that screamed running away and needing almost two weeks to get your head straight before you could go home.

Something bigger troubled her.

Except for the times they'd found radio stations, the inside of the car had been silent. She'd had plenty of time to confide in him. But she hadn't.

When they reached another hotel chain at a stop just off the highway, they got out of the car, registered and went to their rooms.

Showering, he told himself that it was stupid, maybe foolish, to want to hear her full story. Once he dropped her off at her father's vineyard, he'd probably never see her again. At the same time, he thought it was cruel to put her in a car and drive her home, and then not say anything to her beyond "where do you want to eat?" If they'd flown, they could have stayed silent for the hours it would have taken to get to Monroe Vineyards. But driving was a whole different story. The long days of nothing but static-laced music or the whine of tires should be making her crazy enough to talk if only to fill the void, but she kept silent.

He stepped out of the bathroom and put on a pair of his new jeans, a big T-shirt and tennis shoes. They had dinner at the diner beside the hotel, where she focused on eating her salad, not talking, then he went back to his room and fell into a deep, wonderful sleep. He woke refreshed, took another shower, put on clean clothes again and firmly decided Morgan's life was her life. Her decisions were hers to make. He wasn't going to ask her about either.

Just as he was about to pick up his wallet and the rental car keys, his phone rang.

He looked at the caller ID and saw it was Colonel Monroe.

He clicked to answer. "Good morning, Colonel."

"I'd expected to hear from you yesterday."

"Things weren't exactly cut-and-dried with your daughter."

The Colonel sighed heavily. "What did she do?"

Not about to admit how easily she'd duped him, Riccardo turned the conversation in a different direction. "You know she bolted from her wedding for a reason."

"What reason? Seriously? What could be important enough that she'd humiliate herself that way?"

He'd never thought of the fact that a runaway bride humiliated herself. Especially not with Cicely. He'd only seen his side of the story—that two days before his wedding the woman who was supposed to love him told the world she didn't by calling off the wedding. It had been humbling, but worse than that, it had hurt. Hurt to the very core of his being. He'd seen himself as her knight in shining armor. The real prince she was supposed to marry. The guy who would make her life wonderful. And in the end, she'd thrown it all back in his face and left with the man who had crushed her. She'd proved that good guys don't win. Bad guys do.

"You think she humiliated herself?"

"Sure, Charles and I might be left holding the bag, but we're also the ones talking to confused guests. What we're hearing is that everybody thinks she's a little crazy or selfish...or both."

He pictured the small town of Lake Justice,

filled with concerned friends and neighbors, all expressing sympathy to Charles and questioning Morgan's sanity. But he knew Charles had hurt *her*. Now the idiot was sucking up sympathy, at the expense of Morgan's reputation.

"She's got a lot of explaining to do, and I sure as hell hope she's got a reason that doesn't make things worse. She already looks like a fool. Has she said anything?"

Riccardo winced. If she looked like a fool it was because Charles and her dad had made her into one. At least Riccardo wouldn't betray her trust.

"No. She hasn't really said anything."

"This is so not like her. None of it is. She was always so quiet and so quick to do what needed to be done."

Another picture began to fall into place in Riccardo's head. A picture of Morgan taking orders from her famous, powerful dad. Never arguing. Never complaining. Just falling in line.

The sheep metaphor became clearer.

"Maybe it's difficult being given orders by the man who was once secretary of state."

The Colonel laughed. "I know. I do have a tendency to be bossy."

"I wouldn't say that you're bossy. More accustomed to being in command."

"Of the foreign policy for an entire country," he said wistfully. "One word from me could have started World War Three. But it never happened because a good soldier is a diplomat first." He sighed. "And I guess that takes us back to my daughter."

"She wants a little time to think."

"She doesn't have time. We need to issue a statement."

Riccardo's brow furrowed. "Issue a statement?"

"I have business contacts who couldn't stay and wait for her to return and explain herself. So does Charles. The sooner we get something out, the better."

"I'm not sure anybody really cares—"

"*You're* not sure? I didn't send you to be sure. I sent you to bring Morgan home. I need to deal with this, and the best way is to get her out into the charity-ball circuit with Charles so that people stop talking about her."

Totally confused, he said, "You'd send her out with Charles? As if nothing happened? Don't you think that would only start people talking again?"

He laughed. "Well, look at you, giving me advice. How many wars have you averted, son?"

Riccardo grimaced.

"How many kids did you raise?" Without giving Riccardo a chance to answer, he said, "Bring her home." Then he hung up.

Riccardo shoved his phone into his jeans pocket, picked up his wallet and car keys and walked to the hotel-room door, righteous indignation making his blood boil. He thought of Morgan again, living with the Colonel, always coming under his command, and sympathy for her exploded. Worse, her dad wasn't just demanding she return home. He would stick her back with the jackass who had hurt her.

His protective instincts kicked into high gear but he instantly stopped them. He'd already made up his mind that this was Morgan's problem, not his. He couldn't interfere. If that wasn't enough to pull him back, the interests of Ochoa Online were. Mitch had a lot on the line. The Colonel had warned Riccardo about his plan to build his own wine website to compete with OchoaWines.com the night *before* the wedding. Morgan running had actually been good for Mitch and Riccardo because it forced the former secretary of state to offer the one thing, the *only* thing, that would give Riccardo a reason to go after his daughter: an end to his plans. If Riccardo would just go to Vegas and bring Morgan home, the Colonel wouldn't build his competing site.

He had to take her home. No more hemming and hawing around. No more being kind to a woman he really didn't know. He had to fulfill his promise.

He found Morgan in the lobby and they decided to have breakfast at the little diner where they'd eaten the night before. After ordering, he glanced at her angelic face. Serious blue eyes. Pert nose. Full lips. He had to take her home, but he couldn't let her walk totally clueless into the mess she'd find. He had to at least lead her in a direction that would alert her that she needed to be prepared for the worst when she returned to Like Justice.

"I talked to your dad this morning."

She winced. "He's still angry."

"Yes. But he also gave me the idea that some of your guests haven't left yet."

She sighed. "A lot of people decided to use traveling to the wedding as an opportunity to take an early fall vacation, tour the local wineries, that sort of thing." She caught his gaze. "But what you're really telling me is that I'm not going to go home to a private resolution. I'll have an audience."

"You might actually arrive to find a bunch of people waiting with popcorn and soda, hoping to see a show."

She sighed, combed her fingers through her hair and shook her head. "Here I was wondering if I could get ten minutes to talk to Charles without my dad. Now I have to wonder if I'll get any privacy at all."

"You don't think your dad will let you talk to Charles alone?"

"No. That's part of the reason figuring out what to say is so difficult. If I knew I would talk to them separately, I'd say one set of things to Charles and one set to my dad."

"Makes sense."

"But figuring out what to say to them together, or even how to convince my dad to leave the room so I can talk to Charles first…it's almost impossible."

"All the more reason to be prepared with good answers when you get home."

She gaped at him. "Haven't I been telling you that all along!"

Her feistiness made him laugh. "Well, look at you getting all sassy with me. Like you were in Vegas." He pointed at her. "You need to remember this. How you feel. So that when you get home, you can make demands."

"Make demands? To my father?"

"Okay. Maybe not make demands. But tell him what you need."

She laughed. "That sounds good in theory but I doubt it will work. If I can't make him leave the room so I can have a private conversation with the man I thought I was going to marry, I don't see how I can make him realize he's suffocating me. The way I see this playing out, I either have to go back to the way things were, or I have to go out on my own. Which will make him so angry, I'll probably never see him again."

Saddened, Riccardo studied her, finally understanding that was the real reason she was delaying going home. She truly believed she'd either have to go back to being a sheep, or she'd be nothing at all.

"Surely, there are other choices."

"I couldn't even get my way about my own wedding. My dad still sees me as the twelve-year-old I was when my mom died. He always believes he's doing the right thing for me. There's no malice intended. So, of course, he doesn't understand if I disagree. Which is why I rarely disagreed. Until now. Until something inside me froze and just wouldn't let me walk down that aisle."

The waitress arrived with their food and Riccardo thanked her. He waited until she'd completely walked away before he leaned across the table. He might have decided not to interfere, but it wouldn't hurt to give her a little guidance so she'd find the answers herself.

"Maybe walking down the aisle, your subconscious was telling you it was time to grow a pair."

Her mouth fell open. "Is that what you want me to go home and tell my dad? Oh, hi, Dad. I left my wedding because my subconscious was telling me to grow a pair?"

"What's he going to do? Arrest you?"

"Disown me." She picked up a square of toast

to butter it, but put it down again. "Look, all this must seem very funny to you. But it's oddly life-and-death to me. I don't want to lose my dad. I lost my mom. And I don't have aunts or uncles, siblings or cousins. I have no one. I don't want to lose the only other family I have. So, while I appreciate your sentiments, you don't understand. I can't just go home a totally different person. I have to figure out how to behave so that things change but he still accepts me."

"You can't just be yourself?"

She tossed her hands. "I don't even know who *myself* is."

"I think—"

"Don't think. From here on out, just drive. Let me think."

Riccardo said, "Fine," and dug in to his eggs and home fries as if his life depended on it. He'd been working to stay out of her drama, but when he couldn't help giving her advice, his thanks was to be scolded. So, fine. He was out.

CHAPTER FOUR

MORGAN'S CHEST TIGHTENED. She hadn't meant to insult Riccardo. Especially since she wasn't angry with him for making suggestions. She was angry with herself because she honestly could not figure out what to say to her dad or how to say it. In her head, she'd rehearsed something snappy and snarky—not quite as crude as Riccardo's suggestion—but a potent little "Dad, it's my life, and I'm going to live it the way I want."

And she'd pictured her dad frowning. He wouldn't yell. Even if she yelled, he wouldn't. No, no. He'd frown in disappointment. Then tell her something like, "You're choosing to toss away the benefit of all my years of experience."

She'd determined there were six comebacks to that. But her dad would have even better comebacks to all six of those.

Because that's what he'd done for a living for

twelve years: outtalk world leaders, some of the smartest people on the planet.

How was she going to best that?

They finished eating, got into the car and stayed silent for two hours. Morgan used the time to have unsuccessful conversations with her dad in her head until the car made a noise that sounded like a bump.

Riccardo immediately slowed the car.

Bump.

Bump.

Bump.

"Damn."

She gripped the dashboard as Riccardo eased the car off the highway. "What is it?"

"A flat tire."

She glanced at him incredulously. "This is what a flat tire feels like?"

"Yes. We probably ran over something sharp and it took this long for the air to seep out."

"You think we ran over something?"

He peered across the seat at her. "Unless somebody punched it with something sharp on purpose."

She shook her head. "I didn't do that, Mr. Jailer."

"I know." He chuckled. "I haven't let you out of my sight long enough for you to find something sharp and jam it sufficiently into the tread that a tire would go flat. If you'd done it while I was sleeping, the tire would have been flat in the morning."

He turned off the engine, pushed open the door and got out.

He'd actually thought that through? Wondered if she'd be idiot enough to ruin a tire?

She shoved open her car door and scrambled after him. "You still don't trust me!"

He sighed as he pushed the key fob to open the trunk. "It's not my job to trust you. It's my job to get you home. No talking, no thinking, just driving. Remember?"

She combed her fingers through her hair. She'd hated making him angry at breakfast. She wasn't the kind of person who lashed out at anyone. Plus, he'd been good to her. He didn't deserve her anger. "Sorry about that."

He said nothing.

"Really. I don't generally act like this, and I feel bad about insulting you."

He pulled in a breath and studied her for a second. "Okay. Apology accepted. But only because the quiet car this morning about drove me nuts."

"You were bored?"

"Weren't you? We've done nothing but drive and eat for days. It's getting old."

She had a little too much on her mind to be bored, but maybe that was the problem. Maybe if she'd stop thinking, an answer would come.

"I wasn't bored. I was trying to come up with something to say to my dad. But apparently thinking isn't helping, so maybe it's time to talk. Except not about my dad. Surely, there are a million other things we could discuss."

Standing in front of the trunk, he considered that. "You're right. The only time we fight is when we talk about you going home. Better to stay away from that. Agreed?"

"Agreed."

He smiled his acknowledgment and her heart kicked against her ribs. Good grief, he was gorgeous. A Nebraska breeze blew his dark hair across his forehead and above brown eyes that were sharp and curious. Warmth flooded her. She dropped her gaze, but it landed on a full mouth that had her wondering what kissing him would be like.

"Let's see if this thing has a spare." He turned his attention to the car again.

She blew out a quiet sigh of relief that he hadn't seemed to notice the way she was looking at him, before she peeked into the trunk and watched him lift the carpeting to reveal a spare tire and some tools. He dropped the tools and tire on the ground then crouched beside the flat. Using the long shiny thing, he eased off the hubcap.

His broad back stretched his knit shirt to capacity then tapered into a trim waist. His blue jeans encased an absolutely perfect butt.

He peered over his shoulder at her. "Taking notes?"

Her face heated. She hoped he was talking about the tire change and hadn't seen the way she was studying him. "No. But maybe I should. If my dad kicks me out, I might need to be able to do things like this."

She regretted the words the minute they were out of her mouth. Talking about her dad was supposed to be off the table.

He rose, took the second tool and put it under

the car's bumper to raise the tire off the road. Cars drove by but the silence from Riccardo was deafening.

Finally, he said, "No trust fund?"

Glad he'd found a way to redeem the conversation, she admitted something she rarely told anyone. "A healthy one, actually."

"So, you'll probably never have to change your own tire."

He might have great eyes, a mouth she wanted to kiss and a nice butt, but the man was back to insulting her. "Look at the pot calling the kettle black. What do you do for a living that lets you drop work at a moment's notice and traipse around the country ruining other people's privacy?"

"You mean what do I do for Ochoa Online?"

"If that's where you work."

He turned and picked up the third tool, crouched beside the car and began unscrewing the bolts that held the tire in place. "Yes. That's where I work."

She slid her gaze from his broad back to his bottom, along muscular thighs currently holding him balanced in front of the tire he disconnected. He had to be strong not to grunt or groan or even sway.

The cool September air suddenly grew warm again.

She forced herself back into the conversation. "So you own a company?"

"Technically, my cousin Mitch owns Ochoa Online." His attention taken by the tire and the conversation, he didn't even glance at her. She took advantage and ran her gaze along the muscles of his arms as they flexed with every twist of the big wrench.

"I'm the money guy. I create and watch our budgets and five-year plans. I monitor sales. And the minute more than thirty dollars in profit comes in, I invest it."

Her brow furrowed. "Thirty dollars?"

"I was teasing."

Annoyed with herself for being so distracted by the flexing of his muscles that she'd made a dumb mistake, she didn't reply.

After thirty seconds of nothing but the sound of interstate traffic whizzing by, he said, "Probably not a lot of teasing goes on at your dad's dinner parties."

"More than you'd expect." Curious about him, and his connection to her father, Morgan brought back the subject of his job. "So, my dad pays to be on your wine site?"

He rose, reached for the spare and carried it to the car. "No. We list his wine and get a commission on everything he sells through our site."

Wow. No wonder taking her home was so important to him. "You make a lot of money because of him, don't you?"

"People like brands. Status. Especially when it comes to wine. Your dad himself is a brand, the epitome of status."

A breeze ruffled his dark hair again but this time it brought the scent of his aftershave to her. She'd smelled it in the car for days, but right now with him making changing a tire look sexy, as he talked about things that made her realize he was pretty damn smart, she began to wonder about him. Who he was. How loyal he had to be to his cousin to take on the task of bringing home a runaway bride. And good grief, why was such a great-smelling, smart, sexy guy still single?

Flustered by her thoughts while he was blissfully unaware that she was practically lusting after him, she said, "Are you telling me my dad's wines only sell because of his name?"

"Your dad's wines are excellent. Name or no name, he wouldn't get on OchoaWines.com if Mitch didn't like the flavor and quality."

She laughed. "Really? You'd have turned down Colonel Monroe?"

"Not me. Mitch." He twisted the wrench, fastening the bolts for the new tire, causing the muscles of his back to ripple. "He has standards for the products he sells. A reputation for offering only the best. People shop at his sites because they know they don't have to look anywhere else. He has the best. So, he'd turn down Queen Elizabeth if her products didn't meet his standards."

"That would be interesting to see."

"No one's ever turned down your dad?"

She thought for a second. "No. Even when things start going wrong, my dad has the ability to guide any conversation in the direction he wants it to go."

"Which is why you're worried about talking to him."

Because they'd agreed not to discuss this, she simply said, "Yes."

He rose, dusted his hands on his thighs and caught her gaze. "You really think he'd kick you out of his life?"

Part of her wanted to remind him they said they weren't going to talk about her situation. The other part wanted another person to understand so she wouldn't think she was just this side of crazy for not being able to live that way anymore.

The other part won. "Not in the way you're assuming. He wouldn't say, 'That's it, Morgan. You're out of here.' He'd tell me he was disappointed in me and treat me differently, coolly, until I fell in line again."

"That's a hell of a way to live."

"Actually, it was a very easy way to live in some respects. I knew exactly what he wanted from me. A respectful daughter who helped him in his business. In fact, I think the blame for Charles rests as much on me as it does on him. I dated Charles because I knew it was what my dad wanted. He wanted me with Charles. So, I was with Charles."

Riccardo stared at her, a confused expression on his handsome face. "That's just sad."

The wind raised her hair and she tucked it behind her ear. "No. It was life with my father. Walking down the aisle, I realized I wanted more."

"More?"

She almost blurted out that she wanted somebody like him. Someone strong and interesting. Someone who listened to her opinions. Gave her choices. But after running away from her wedding, another man was the last thing on her mind. As it was, if her dad shut her out, she'd have to create an entire new life, without family, and probably with only a handful of friends who'd be okay with going against her dad. She didn't need the added complication of this handsome Spanish guy.

But, oh, he was tempting.

"I don't know how to describe *more* except to say I realized I'd never had the chance to see who I am. What I'd do if I didn't have one of the smartest men on the planet making my decisions for me before I even knew there were decisions to be made."

"I think I get it. Your dad looked down the board, knew he'd want grandkids, found a suitable guy and introduced him into your world."

"That's it exactly!"

He picked up the old tire.

Happy he understood, she bent over to gather the tools. "It's like you were in our living room."

He tossed the tire into the trunk and took the tools from her. "I know a bit about bossy patriarchs. Mitch and I are modern thinkers, but our dads aren't. Our granddad was worse." He looked up at her. "It's why Nanna's so strong. Not opinionated, but strong."

"Your grandmother, right?"

"Yes. She was married to a guy two generations above me. My father and Uncle Santiago are strong, but apparently their father was like a stubborn bull."

"My dad's not a bull, but he's stubborn. But not like you'd think. He doesn't dig in his heels and fight. He has this look."

She tried to imitate her father's expression when he was unhappy with something she said.

Riccardo shook his head. "Sorry. That wouldn't get me to change my mind."

"How about this one?" She raised one eyebrow as she squinted.

"I'd probably offer him a laxative."

"Stop!" A laugh escaped her. "I don't want to

make fun of my dad. I just want to show you that he can be intimidating."

"I already know that."

She nodded. "That's right. He got you to come after me by threatening to pull out of your company."

"Among other things."

"He knows how to find a weakness and exploit it."

"So, you have to figure out how to be strong. Sometimes it isn't what you say but how you say it." He closed the trunk and said, "'Dad, thank you very much for the benefit of your experience but I've decided to go in another direction.'"

She sighed. "He'd pour a brandy, offer me a seat on a Queen Anne chair by the fireplace in the den and ask me to explain the direction."

"And you'd say, 'I'm not ready to reveal particulars yet.'"

She deepened her voice, imitating her dad. "'It sounds to me that you haven't thought it through.'"

He raised his voice an octave to sound like a woman. "'Nope. I'm good. Say, did you see the Patriots won another game?'"

She laughed. Really laughed. "He'd know I was deflecting and just bring the conversation back."

"And you deflect again. Until he can't remember what you were talking about."

She gazed up at him. "I wish it was that simple."

"I'm not saying that you'd get it right the first time. You'd need to practice."

"Like in a mirror?"

"You could do that. But the best practice would be engaging in conversations with him. See what works. Toss what doesn't."

"I can't do that. I have to set things straight as soon as I get home." She swiped her windblown hair across her face and behind her ear again. "I don't want to give him the impression that things can go back to the way they were. I want to have the conversation the minute I see him. But that just confuses things because I also need to talk to Charles. I have this horrible feeling that I'll be in on this dual discussion, talking to Charles about breaking up and my dad about our future. And nobody will hear me. It'll be a mess."

"I thought you said your dad was leaving for Stockholm?"

"He is. Two days after my honeymoon was supposed to be over."

"So, go home after he's gone. Talk to Charles first, then talk to him."

She stared at him. "That's brilliant." The wind blew her hair across her face and she whisked it away again.

"You got some dust on your face."

He brushed his finger along her cheek and Morgan's heart stuttered. The whole world seemed to stop. The touch had been as gentle as the breeze, but it had the power to steal her breath. Add that to him standing so close, smelling fantastic, looking even better and actually listening to her, and her brain almost couldn't process it.

With their gazes locked and the sound of the interstate a dull hum behind them, her heart beat so hard she swore she could feel it. She'd give every cent in her considerable trust fund to be able to kiss him.

"There's another reason to delay going home. If you go back now, he's going to have you go out into the charity-ball circuit with Charles."

All thought of kissing him fled. "What?"

"He thinks that's damage control."

Fury roared through her. "That's insanity!"

"He's saying it's a way to stave off gossip."

"It's a way to get me back with Charles!" She tossed her hands and stomped away, yelling, "Damn! Damn! Damn!"

A car suddenly pulled up behind them. The driver rolled down his window and called, "Everything okay here?"

"Yes! We're fine," Riccardo answered. "Flat tire. We fixed it."

The older man nodded toward her. "Everything okay with your friend?"

Riccardo laughed. "Yes. She just got bad news."

"Okay." The man pulled his gearshift out of Park. "You should stop at the next town to make sure there's enough air in the spare."

"Will do!"

The man drove off and Morgan just stared at calm, casual Riccardo. Had she been with her dad, she would have been embarrassed that a car had stopped because she was having a fit. With Riccardo she didn't even feel a blip of discomfort. And neither did he. It didn't bother him that she yelled, tossed her hands, even stomped a little. He hadn't called her unladylike. Hadn't reminded her people could see.

The strangest sense filled her. For as sexy and smart and fascinating as he was, he was also very calm and collected. She didn't have to be on guard or on her best behavior around him. She was with, arguably, the best-looking, sexiest man she'd ever met, and she was comfortable.

That thought brought her up short.

Comfortable? The man had virtually kidnapped her. And the way he looked at her had made her want to kiss him.

Kiss him.

She didn't know what she was feeling around him, but it sure as hell wasn't comfortable.

They did stop at the next town. Riccardo checked them into a hotel so she could take a break while he had the tire inspected at a garage. She showered, put on a clean outfit and watched mindless TV as she waited for his call. When her room phone finally rang, they decided to get dinner after he showered.

She combed her hair and primped a bit, making herself look the best she could in cheap jeans, telling herself she was not trying to be attractive for him. She just wanted to look her best.

Eventually, he called again and he instructed her to meet him in the lobby so they could walk to the restaurant beside the hotel.

When she got to the reservation desk, he already stood there, handsome in his new jeans and plain blue shirt and smelling like someone sent straight from heaven.

As they walked to the nearby restaurant, she reminded herself that she still had a fiancé. Reminded herself that this guy making her feel things she never felt before was also carting her home to her dad. She couldn't be comfortable or happy around him. She had to stay focused.

Riccardo's steak sizzled as the waitress set it in front of him.

Morgan glanced at it longingly. "That sounds delicious."

"I know it will be." He peered at her salad. "You really should eat more red meat."

She poked at a piece of bacon. "This is kind of red."

He chuckled. "You have an interesting sense of humor."

She wished she could just say thanks. But the truth was she wasn't anything like the person she'd been with him for the past few days.

"No, I don't. With you I just sort of say what jumps into my head. That's why you laugh. But most of it is meaningless."

"Everything in life doesn't have to have meaning. Otherwise, we'd all be extremely serious and extremely tired."

"I had been!" She hadn't meant to say that. Once again, it had just popped out and she said it because she was comfortable with him, when she shouldn't be.

She squeezed her eyes shut. "See what I mean?"

"You were being honest. Isn't that what you're trying to do? Find the real you? The honest one?"

"I didn't realize I'd have to be a bumbling idiot to find her."

"You're not a bumbling idiot. You're normal. Normal conversation ebbs and flows. Sometimes people say things that sound funnier when they come out than the person had intended. Sometimes people blurt things out by instinct." He reached across the table and took her hand. "But that's how the person you're talking to actually gets to know you."

She pulled her lower lip between her teeth. He probably thought she was thinking that through. The truth was, the feeling of his big hand wrapped around hers sent warmth cascading through her. He was gorgeous. Sexy. Honest. Real. And so easy to talk to. She longed to open up completely, tell him every darned thing in her life, then kiss him senseless.

Which was insane. Ridiculous. Riccardo Ochoa wasn't merely taking her back to her dad, she also had Charles at home. Somebody she'd thought she'd loved, but she didn't. She shouldn't even *want* to get involved with another man.

She *didn't* want to get involved with another man.

She was simply really, really attracted to Riccardo.

Physically.

It had to be nothing more than a physical attraction. She didn't know him well enough for what she felt to be deeper. And he most certainly didn't have the kindness and compassion she kept attributing to him. Otherwise, he wouldn't be taking her back to her father.

For once, she was glad he'd stuck to his guns taking her home. It proved he wasn't the nice guy she believed. He was a man with a mission. She was just a means to an end for him.

As long as she remembered that, the physical attraction she felt for him would fade.

Riccardo saw the battle in her eyes and immediately changed the subject. How she handled her life wasn't his concern, but she was so lost it was hard not to offer her counsel. Still, it was wrong. Especially when the things he'd just told her only seemed to confuse her more.

They finished dinner making polite conversation about Mitch, his websites, Mitch's new wife, Lila, and Lila's mom, Francine. At age ten, Lila had told a social worker about her mom's alcohol abuse and she'd been shuffled into foster care and gotten lost in the system. She and her mom hadn't seen each other in fifteen years and Mitch had been instrumental in bringing them together.

Riccardo had told the story to have something to talk about that could take him and Morgan through dinner and the walk back to the hotel, but watching her face in the elevator back to their side-by-side rooms, he knew the story had affected her.

"I lost my mom at twelve and she lost her mom at ten?"

"Yes." He wouldn't have told her Lila's story if he'd remembered how old Morgan had been when her mom died. But maybe it was good that he hadn't. It was the first normal curiosity he'd seen in her eyes since this trip began. Though her story and Lila's were different, they'd both lost their moms.

"So how did Lila end up?"

"Happy. She works for us. Her mom, too. They had some open, honest conversations, but the bottom line was they had missed each other." He paused. "No, I think they longed for each other. That's why they didn't quit when the discussions got difficult. I was proud of them both."

The elevator doors opened but she didn't get out. Instead, her head tilted and she studied him. "Are you really this emotional?"

"Excuse me?"

"You really seem to get emotional about other people's problems."

He directed her out of the elevator. "First off, Spaniards call it passionate. Second, look who you're comparing me to. A dad who constantly manipulated you to get his own way, and a guy who had to have an older friend fix him up with his daughter. Of course you see me as being emotional. You've lived in a world with two duds for a decade."

Morgan laughed then squeezed her eyes shut as if she hated admitting it, but she said, "True."

"And Charles didn't stop there," Riccardo said, enjoying her laughter. When she laughed, her tension left. The confusion in her eyes dimmed. And he didn't have to regret his part in taking her home. "Oh, no. He went all the way and let his older friend groom him."

"Um, take a look in front of you." She laughed again. "I can't even figure out how to explain running from my wedding. It's not as if I was such a great prize myself."

"You are a great prize." The words came out soft and filled with regret that her dad had skewed the way she saw herself.

She stopped at her door, but she didn't use her key card to open it. She glanced at Riccardo, her pale pink face illuminated by the light beside her door. "I'm a twenty-five-year-old woman who doesn't know who she is."

"You have to know you're beautiful."

She caught his gaze. Her long black lashes blinked over sad blue eyes. "Physical things fade."

"You're pretty in here," he countered, touching her chest just above the soft swell of her breasts. "When you're sixty, eighty, a hundred, you'll still be compassionate."

She shook her head. "You don't know that. We just met. Aside from the fact that I ran from my wedding and my dad's a bit of a control freak, you don't know much of anything about me."

"I know that you connected with Lila's story and felt bad for both Lila and her mom."

"Because I understood."

"Other people dismiss Francine as being selfish, weak. Most are sad for Lila. You felt sorry for both."

"There are two sides to every story."

"And maybe that's what you need to tell your dad."

As she thought that through, the air around them stilled. She swung her long blond hair over her shoulder. Her head tilted and she smiled. "You know what? Maybe it is."

Silence hung between them as they stared into each other's eyes. The warmth in her big blue orbs touched his heart, but the lift of her lips sparked a small fire in his belly. Everything male inside him awoke. The urge to kiss her tumbled through him.

Fighting it, he forced himself to return her smile, though he had to clear his throat before he could speak. "Good. Think it through on the drive tomorrow, while I'm listening to country music, counting the bugs that die on the windshield."

She laughed.

He should have turned, walked the few steps to his own room and gone inside. Gotten away from her. Instead, he stayed right where he was.

"I wish I had time to meet Lila before I had to talk to my dad. If nothing else she might be able to give me a nice ice-breaker line."

He wished he could comb his fingers through

her long yellow hair. "You have the oddest sense of humor."

"And in a way, it's interesting to experiment with it." She caught his gaze. "Particularly since it seems like you don't judge."

"I don't."

"How do you do that?" Her eyes told him that this was important to her. Probably because she'd grown up in a house with nothing but judgment.

He shrugged. "I let you be you. It's been sort of fun watching you root around, trying to find yourself." Because the more layers she peeled back, the more he liked her. Really liked her. Not just in a sexual way, but as a person.

The urge to kiss her set his instincts in motion. His upper body leaned forward. His head began to descend—

He jerked himself to a stop.

What the hell was he doing?

Angry with himself, he pulled back and rubbed his hand along his nape, avoiding her eyes. All this time he'd been feeling an attraction, but he'd been confident that he'd never follow through because she was sweet. And he liked sexy. Yet, somehow, she'd managed to merge the two.

Because he'd been helping her. Talking to her. Growing to like her.

Just as he'd done with Cicely.

He took another step back. "I'll see you in the morning."

She smiled that smile again. The one that had shifted his definition of sexy to include everything that she was. "Okay."

He said a quiet "Okay," and walked to the room beside hers as she used her key card to open her door and disappear behind it.

Memories of falling in love with Cicely crept into his brain. This time, he didn't try to stop them. Not because he wanted to remember the humiliation, but because he needed to remember that sometimes his urge to be a knight in shining armor blinded him to the truth.

And the truth was Morgan didn't want to go home. Yes, she said it was because she wasn't ready to face her father. But that only made her desire to escape stronger. She might not bolt in God-knew-where Nebraska, but once they got closer to Chicago she'd have plenty of chances to run. Especially if his guard was down because he was beginning to like her.

He tossed his key card on the dresser, thankful they only had another few days of driving. The closer they got to Chicago, the more he would watch her.

Just as he convinced himself he could keep it all under control, his phone rang. Glancing at the caller ID, he groaned. He squeezed his eyes shut for five seconds before he popped them open and answered.

"Good evening, Colonel."

"I expected my daughter to be home by now."

"I told you we were driving—"

"And I told you I wanted her home! *Driving* wasn't the order I gave you! I want her on a plane *now*."

That's when it all came together in Riccardo's head. *This* was the guy Morgan knew she'd be talking to when she returned to Lake Justice. No matter how many times she called her dad a diplomat, the Colonel that Riccardo kept encountering was a hothead. Her confidence would shatter when confronted by this angry, manipulative man, the man she didn't want to lose from her life because she'd already lost her mom. He was her family. She wanted to keep him. Yet, the

Colonel knew how to push her buttons and Riccardo was certain he'd use every weapon at his disposal to get her to fall in line.

He paced to the bathroom as two options hung before him. Save himself and tell the Colonel she'd be on a plane tomorrow. Or save her. Which meant she could try to escape when they got close to Chicago. It also meant more time together. More time for her to tempt him.

Except now that he had his bearings, she wouldn't tempt him anymore. He could be as stubborn as her father. He did not have to worry.

"Did you hear me, son? I want her home tomorrow!"

Riccardo's last remaining piece of knight in shining armor rose in him. It was small, but it was powerful. He could not send Morgan home until she was ready. And he wasn't an idiot. He would not make the mistake he'd made with Cicely twice.

"Respectfully, Colonel, Morgan will be home when she gets home."

Then *he* hung up the phone.

He perched on the lip of the bathtub and ran his hands down his face. He might have saved Morgan, but he'd also taken the first step that assured the Colonel would dump OchoaWines.com, create his own wine site and sweet-talk their clients away from them.

He worked out the numbers in his head. An undertaking like creating a monster website and stealing a hundred clients wouldn't happen over a weekend or even a week. Also, Mitch didn't get back to New York for another week. So Riccardo had a little time to play with.

And he *would* eventually take Morgan home. She just needed a few more days to bolster her confidence.

But not in the car. Not getting close to Chicago, where she could potentially ditch him—

An idea leaped into his brain and his head snapped up. She needed someone to talk to? Nanna was smart and strong. Strong was her middle name. And then there was his mom. Also a smart woman. Those were the people she should be talking with. Not a jaded playboy, who found her so attractive he was having trouble keeping his hands off her, but two women who knew how to deal with demanding men.

CHAPTER FIVE

MORGAN SHOWERED THEN put on a T-shirt and slid into bed. She tried to sleep, but she couldn't stop thinking about Riccardo.

He'd almost kissed her. He might think she hadn't noticed, but she had, because the same feelings were running through her. And this time it wasn't just physical. Riccardo Ochoa was a wonderful person. She'd been seeing it all along. But tonight, his goodness had somehow connected with her attraction and the way she'd felt had been gloriously scary.

Remembering those thirty seconds as his head was descending toward hers made her breath shimmy. Every cell in her body had been ready for the touch of his lips on hers. But he hadn't taken that last step, hadn't kissed her, because it was wrong.

He might be unlike anybody she knew—unafraid to talk, wise about family and relationships and amazingly good-looking—but she still had a fiancé at home. Until she dealt with Charles, she shouldn't be attracted to anybody, let alone kissing somebody.

Her room phone rang and she almost jumped out of her skin. Thinking it might be Riccardo, she grabbed for the receiver, but just as quickly yanked back her hand.

She should not be excited to talk to him.

The phone rang again.

But she was.

She squeezed her eyes shut. This was a mess.

The phone rang a third time and she reminded herself that if Riccardo was calling it was probably for something about their trip. She very cautiously answered it. "Hello."

"Good evening, Ms. Monroe. This is the front desk. Mr. Ochoa left a wake-up call for you for tomorrow morning at seven. You need to approve it."

Relief flooded her. "Yes. Yes. It's fine. Thank you."

"Thank you and have a good evening."

She hung up the phone a bit confused about why Riccardo hadn't called her himself, but glad he hadn't. His not wanting direct communication said he didn't have feelings for her—

Or he could have just called the front desk and given the wake-up call order for both of them because it was convenient, and the hotel had a policy that said the clerk taking the call had to follow up.

His feelings for her weren't neutral. The man had almost kissed her. And her feelings for him weren't neutral, either. She'd wanted him to kiss her.

She turned off the bedside lamp and settled under the covers, forcing her mind off Riccardo, and it jumped to Charles.

Here she was attracted to a man—no matter how foolishly—and she hadn't even really broken up with Charles.

Guilt consumed her. Though she was fairly certain he would realize her running from the church meant they were through, the need to make it official pounded through her.

She sat up and clicked on the lamp again. Lifting her cell phone from the bedside table, she didn't let herself think about the time difference, didn't consider that Charles might be with her dad. She simply dialed his cell number and waited until he answered.

"Hello." A quick pause. "Who is this?"

His voice was thick and groggy. She did the calculations in her head and realized it was after midnight in Lake Justice, and he was in bed. But in a way, that was good. It meant he was nowhere near her father.

"I'm sorry, Charles. It's me. Morgan."

"Morgan." His voice was instantly stronger, as if he'd come to attention. "Where are you?"

"That's not important." She didn't want to have a long, drawn-out conversation. She just wanted to apologize and make sure he understood she wasn't coming back to him—wasn't going out on the charity-ball circuit to smooth things over. She couldn't be attracted to Riccardo then go home and pretend nothing had happened. Lots had happened. Too much for her to tell Charles, and maybe too much for it to be his concern anyway.

She knew they'd have to talk again, more seriously—especially about selling the condo they'd bought and returning gifts—but they could have that discussion when she got home. For now, she simply needed to end it.

"Look, I'm really sorry for everything. Running. Leaving you to deal with the mess. But I know you probably realized that my running from our wedding meant there was a problem."

She expected him to say something like, "Nothing we can't fix." Instead, he softly said, "Yes. It's kind of hard to ignore a woman who'd rather go on the lam than marry you."

"I'm so sorry. Everything just closed in on me."

"And we did have the fight the day before."

Relief filled her lungs with air again. He sounded like he more than understood. He sounded like someone who'd adjusted. "Yes. We did."

"It took me 'til yesterday for it to sink in, but I got it. The toast from my best man didn't bother you because it made you think I didn't love you, but because it prompted you to realize you didn't love me."

Her breath caught. His level of understanding amazed her. Surprised her a bit, too, since it had taken her two days in Vegas and a few on the road to come to that conclusion.

"Our dating and engagement all fell together so easily, so pat, that I don't think I ever really took the time to figure out what I felt."

He sighed. "I get it. And I'm okay. Your dad's another story, though."

"I know."

"You're going to have your hands full when you get home."

She winced. She might be settling some things with Charles, but her biggest problem still remained. "I know that, too."

The conversation died. Twenty seconds ticked off the clock. He drew a breath. "So, this is it?"

"Yeah." Her heart drooped a little bit. "I hope we can still be friends."

He laughed. "Women always say that."

"That's because we have to like someone as a friend to even consider marrying him."

"Yeah. Right." He took another quick breath. "Look, I have to go. Can I tell your dad you're fine?"

He might have adjusted, but he was still her dad's errand boy.

But it wouldn't hurt for him to tell her dad she was okay. "Yes. Sure. Tell him I'm fine."

Another silence, then Charles softly said, "Goodbye, Morgan."

"Goodbye, Charles."

She hung up the phone, a sense of relief filling her. Charles might not have been the man of her dreams, but he was a good person. And she'd done the right thing by calling him.

She turned off the lamp and settled on her pillow again, but the strangest feeling suddenly hit her. She was free.

Free.

No longer engaged. Not under her dad's thumb. Her own person for the first time since she was twelve.

And traveling with a man who tempted her.

The next morning, Riccardo waited for Morgan at the registration desk of the hotel. When she arrived, she barely looked at him. And who could blame her? He'd almost kissed her the night before. She'd have to be a total idiot not to have seen it.

She wasn't in the state of mind to have a fling. And he was about to defy her father—to take her to Spain rather than take her home. He didn't want to have another Cicely on his hands. But he wasn't going to let Morgan go back to Lake Justice until she was ready. So, he had to be smart.

He was being smart. Taking her to his nanna to get the help she really needed.

They checked out, and as they walked to the lobby door, he said, "Give me your phone."

She glanced up at him. "Why?"

"Do you know phones can be used to track people?"

"Yes."

"Well, last night I told your dad we'd be home when we got home. I don't think he took it too well."

She shot him a curious look.

"He was angry enough that he might send someone after us. We have to get rid of anything he can use to find us."

He dropped their phones into a trash can just outside the hotel door. They walked up to the Mercedes and he patted the hood. "Including this."

She peered across the black car hood at him. "We're going to stop driving?"

"Yes."

Her eyes widened. "We're gonna walk?"

He laughed. "No. We're just going somewhere we can stay for a few days."

She peeked at him. "I've always loved Chicago."

"I was thinking more about Spain."

Her confused expression became downright pained. "Spain?"

"My family's vineyard. You can meet my mom and nanna, watch how our families interact. Watch how I relate to my dad. Or better, watch how my cousin Alonzo's wife, Julia, relates to her dad. He owns a vineyard, too."

She gaped. "Really? You think I'm so bad I need examples of normal behavior?"

"No, but I think a couple of days around a real family—a big family, counting Nanna as the matriarch and my dad and his brother and their families—would give you some perspective. You say you want to think things through? Vineyards are beautiful in Spain. And quiet. That's where you need to be."

Morgan gaped at him.

The man had almost kissed her the night before. *Almost kissed her.*

And now he was taking her to Spain to meet his family?

The obvious jumped into her head. That he liked her enough to want her to meet his family, but she quickly crossed that off with a big red marker. They'd known each other for a few days. And he *hadn't* kissed her. He'd pulled back. If he was taking her across an ocean, it wasn't for romance, but to make sure her dad didn't find her before he left for Stockholm.

That was a good thing. If she could wait until after he left for Stockholm before she went home, she could talk to Charles first and have another few days to get her bearings before she had to explain to her dad that their relationship had to change.

Hiding out in Spain was not such a bad idea.

She sucked in a breath. "Okay, Marco. Let's go."

He glared at her across the car hood. "Marco Polo was not Spanish."

She laughed. "Right."

"I'm mean it. No more calling me that."

She studied his big dark eyes. "You take your heritage very seriously."

He directed her into the Mercedes. "If you think I'm bad, wait 'til you meet the family."

He got behind the steering wheel as she slid into the passenger seat. Calm as always, sexy as hell, he started the car and she couldn't help wondering what it would be like to be meeting his family for real, as his girlfriend.

The returning thought shocked her so much that it jarred her demanding father out of her head and started a whole new chain of thoughts. She was a runaway bride. His family was old-school, steeped in tradition. They would probably think her absolutely crass.

But she didn't really have anywhere else to go. She had three hundred dollars. Without her credit cards, she was sunk. And going to Spain was the perfect plan. She sincerely doubted her dad would find her there.

As they returned the Mercedes to a rental-car agency and Riccardo called a friend and arranged to use his jet, her thoughts went around and around. By the time the plane was ready for them, she was still nervous. But she didn't want to talk about this with Riccardo. She'd already behaved like a crazy woman with him. It was time to start keeping some of her thoughts to herself.

Luckily, the stress and constant travel of the

past few days caught up with her, and five minutes after the jet was in the air, she fell asleep and didn't wake up until the pilot's announcement that they should fasten their seat belts for the landing.

Noting the warm cover tucked around her, she felt incredibly guilty. "Sorry."

Riccardo shook his head. "Don't be sorry. I slept most of the flight myself. Besides, you'll be glad you slept. When we land it will be a little past eight in the morning."

"I slept sixteen hours!"

"No. There's a time difference between the US and Spain. Besides, you clearly needed the sleep. Nothing to worry about."

She pulled her bottom lip under her teeth. There was a lot to worry about. A thoughtful guy like this had to come from a nice family. Two weeks ago, she would have charmed their socks off. Now, she'd left a groom at the altar and was hiding out from her dad.

"Your family's going to think I'm crazy."

The jet began its descent. "Not hardly."

"Seriously?"

He shrugged. "Have you ever heard the story of

why Mitch started his company in the US rather than Spain?"

"No."

"Mitch's brother, Alonzo, stole his girlfriend."

Her eyebrows rose. "Oh."

"Mitch had been angling to start Ochoa Online for years, but his father, Santiago, would never give the go-ahead. Then all hell broke loose when Mitch found Alonzo and Julia in his bedroom."

Morgan about swallowed her tongue. That made running from her wedding look like small potatoes. "That's awful!"

"It was." He leaned across his seat a bit, getting closer, as if telling her a secret. "They swore nothing had happened. That Mitch had actually walked in on their first kiss, but Santiago was so afraid the scandal would split the family apart that he decided Mitch needed to go away and he offered the start-up capital for the business."

Morgan pressed her lips together to keep from laughing. "Oh…that's—"

"Scandalous. I know."

She laughed and lightly slapped his forearm. "Stop acting like this upsets you. You're loving telling this story."

His eyes sparkled. "I am."

Morgan swallowed. She could drown in the humor in his dark, dark eyes. And maybe that was the real reason for the anxiety tripping through her. She shouldn't be going anywhere with this man who tempted her, let alone across an ocean. But here she was, on a jet, landing in Spain.

She took a breath to clear those thoughts, because it was too late to do anything about it now. "Then what happened?"

"Mitch told his dad he would only leave if the money Santiago provided for OchoaWines.com would be a loan, not an investment."

"That doesn't sound so bad."

"Santiago might not be Colonel Monroe, but he's a family patriarch. He wanted Mitch's business to be part of the family's enterprises."

"And your cousin didn't?"

"He saw an opportunity. In his mind, he was giving up everything. The price was autonomy. And he paid all the money back. With interest. So the family lost nothing."

"Clever."

His smile warmed. "So, Mitch goes to America and creates Ochoa Online and does what no one guessed he would do. He adds other wines to the site. Santiago flipped. Mitch reminded him it was his company, not the family's, and *that* argument got so big everybody forgot that Alonzo stole Julia from him."

After half her childhood of being raised with only a father, and no other family, the magnitude of what that fight must have been like nearly overwhelmed her. "I'm not quite sure I'm ready for your family."

"The trouble is long past. Mitch gives Ochoa Vineyards the prime spot on his website and doesn't take a commission from their sales. He makes a ton of money for the family. Plus, he got married a few weeks ago."

She nodded. "To Lila."

"Yes."

"The woman who spent her childhood in foster care because she got lost in the system."

"Yes."

"Wow, you people are like a soap opera."

"Not really. We're just family. I told you all that so you would see my family will barely bat an eyelid when they meet you. We have our own skeletons."

The plane landed. They waited quietly for the pilot and copilot to come out of the cockpit and open the door.

Though she felt a little cheap and tawdry after hearing that story, Morgan's interest in meeting Riccardo's family had about quadrupled.

The copilot walked out, opened the door that lowered the stairs and wished them a good day in Spanish. Fluent in that language—and three others—Morgan thanked him, then walked out of the jet and stepped into a world of green covered by the most amazing blue sky.

A limo awaited them beside the hangar of the private airstrip. As she and Riccardo walked toward it, the driver opened the back door and Morgan saw an older woman sitting on one of the two bench seats that faced each other.

Riccardo said, "That's Nanna."

Small, classically beautiful with black hair with ribbons of gray streaking through and bright dark eyes, Riccardo's nanna didn't look anything like any grandmother Morgan knew.

After they got settled on the seat across from her, his nanna handed Riccardo a glass of red. "I miss you like the sun in winter."

And she didn't talk like anyone Morgan knew, either. She was sultry. Intriguing.

"Very funny, Nanna." Riccardo laughed. "You miss Mitch more."

Nanna sighed eloquently. "You boys. Always a competition." She faced Morgan with a smile. "And this must be Morgan Monroe."

"She's the daughter of—"

"Colonel Monroe." Nanna sized her up in one quick glance. "You ran from your wedding."

Morgan said, "Yes, ma'am," as Riccardo said, "Nanna!"

Nanna looked totally unrepentant. "What? You already told me all that. Besides, I'm an old woman. I might not live long enough to rehash the basics and Miss Monroe looks like someone who appreciates candor."

Considering his family had bigger, better secrets, Morgan didn't mind talking about her own indiscretion. "I also don't want to tiptoe around the subject. So, here's the story. I got halfway down the aisle, realized I was making a mistake and got myself on the commuter to JFK before anyone could stop me."

Nanna laughed. "I'd have paid to see that. I bet your dad is angry."

Riccardo mumbled, "He is." Then he looked out the window.

Morgan's heart gave a funny catch. He was pulling himself out of the conversation, more or less handing her over to his grandmother—

She suddenly realized the real reason he'd brought her to Spain. He was on the hook with her dad. Responsible for her. Yet they'd gotten so close in just a few days that he'd almost kissed her. Getting involved with her would be like professional suicide. He'd brought her to Spain so she'd have his family to entertain her, and he wouldn't have to worry about what was growing between them.

Disappointment began to rise but she stopped it. She didn't want to get involved with him, either. She was only a few days out of the most serious relationship of her life. She did not want to be falling for another man.

Putting distance between them was the right thing to do.

So, she let him stare out the window on his side, and she turned to look out the window on hers.

The morning sun glistened off the dewy grass beside the road that threaded through the valley.

Nanna pointed at the rows and rows of green leaves that Morgan knew sheltered their grapes. "We started off as one vineyard and got lucky enough to buy the neighbor's." She poured Morgan a glass of wine. "We combined them and now we have an empire almost as big as your dad's." She smiled. "Bigger if you count what Mitch and Riccardo have done with their online presence."

Taking the wine, Morgan laughed. "*You're* the one who's competitive."

Nanna smiled. "I prefer to be called feisty." She turned to Riccardo. "So, you came home to help with the grapes?"

That brought his gaze back from the window. "The grapes?"

"It's about to be harvest time." She laughed. "Surely you haven't been away so long you've forgotten. I expect Alonzo to announce it's time to pick any day now."

Morgan glanced at the seemingly endless fields of grapes. It would take hundreds of people to get all this harvested on time. "You pick by hand?"

Riccardo glanced at her. "Yes."

She held her breath, caught in the gaze of his captivating brown eyes. Of all the things Morgan had thought might happen in her life, falling for a stranger was not one of them. Sexy or not. Handsome or not.

These feelings she had were so far out of her comfort zone that she worried running from her wedding had changed her too much. Morgan Monroe, the real Morgan Monroe, did not fall for strangers.

She faced Nanna again. "Up until a few years ago, my dad had our grapes picked by hand, too. I've helped."

Nanna clapped her hands. "Excellent! We get lots of laborers from town." She leaned close to Morgan. "Even some tourists volunteer. But everyone in the family also picks." She flicked a glance at Riccardo.

Riccardo said, "It'll be fun," though he sounded less than enthusiastic.

Nanna didn't seem to care. "Yes, it will be." She smiled at Morgan. "Have you brought a gown?"

The quick change of topic made Morgan blink. "A gown?"

"There'll be a ball when Mitch and Lila return."

"I barely brought any clothes. I'm not even sure I have enough underwear."

Nanna's musical laugh echoed through the limo. "No problem. I love to shop. Let's get you settled in then you and I will head into town." She frowned. "You do have a credit card, right?"

She winced. "I tossed them in Vegas when I realized my dad could find me by watching my purchases."

Riccardo pulled his wallet from his pants pocket. "Here. Company card. Spend as much as you like. We can expense it."

Nanna clapped with glee. "We are going to have such fun."

Riccardo held back a grimace. He was happy Nanna liked Morgan, but his afternoon would not be fun. He might not have kissed the runaway bride in his custody, but he almost had. If he had, his explanation to Mitch for why he'd refused to take her home would have been infinitesimally worse. Especially since he wasn't 100 percent sure he wasn't doing what he'd done with Cicely—falling for a woman who might not have feelings for him, as much as she needed him.

He thanked God he'd stepped back from that kiss, and determined with every fiber of his being to get this situation back on track. First, get Morgan settled with his nanna. Second, come up with an explanation for Mitch about why she was in Spain instead of Lake Justice. Third, let Nanna guide her on what to say to her father to get her life back.

He turned to Nanna. "When is Mitch expected?"

"He didn't pin down a time. But the ball is Friday next week. They promised to be here a few days before that."

That gave Morgan time to get her bearings. She could even meet Lila and go to the ball. And after that, her dad would leave for Stockholm and she could go home.

The driver pulled the limo onto the lane for Ochoa Vineyards, toward the original stone mansion. Built centuries ago, it was a great two-story house, beautiful even. But if the transfixed expression on Morgan's face was anything to go by, she saw far more.

"It's gorgeous. Like time stood still."

"Not on the inside," Nanna commented casually. "The first floor has been renovated to be the business offices for the vineyard, along with a lovely gift shop." She leaned in close to Morgan. "There's a huge ballroom in the back with its own entrance. The basement is our restaurant. We only serve dinner. And the second floor has two apartments. One for me. One for Marguerite and Santiago, Mitch's parents."

"Wow."

Nanna took Morgan's hand and led her out of the limo. "I'll bet the home of your vineyard is every bit as lovely."

"It's nice," Morgan agreed, as Riccardo climbed out behind her. "But there's not a lot of charm. It's stuffy." She glanced at the big house. "Look at the lines in the stone. This house seems like it's been here forever, lovingly guarding its occupants."

Nanna slipped her arm across Morgan's shoulders and gave her a quick hug. "That's exactly how I see it."

The driver opened the trunk to get their baggage, such as it was. When Nanna saw Riccardo's duffel and Morgan's small black suitcase, she clicked her tongue. "Seriously, you and I are going shopping as soon as we get you settled."

She hooked Morgan's arm with her own and guided her down the cobblestone sidewalk that led first to a duplex and then to Ochoa Vineyard's newly constructed condos.

Riccardo said, "I see the building is done."

"Yes. Lucky for you," Nanna said over her shoulder. "Alonzo and Julia are in the one side of the duplex and Mitch and Lila will be taking up the other. Poor Francine has been staying with Santiago and Marguerite."

It was why the family had decided to build eight condos. With Mitch getting married and Lila's mom being folded into the clan, their group was growing. Add other guests and businessmen and women who came and went, and they needed more space.

Following Nanna and Morgan, Riccardo said, "We'll be the first to stay in the new condos?"

"Yes. Francine will be returning to New York with Lila and Mitch. It seemed foolish to move her over for only a few days." Nanna tossed him a puzzled frown. "I thought you'd go to your parents' house?"

His parents' home at the second vineyard was only two miles down the road, but as sympathetic as he'd become to Morgan's problems, he hadn't forgotten how easily she'd duped him in Vegas. His plan might have been to bring her to Spain so he could get some distance from her, but he didn't think it was a good idea to be two miles away. Just in case she got it in her head that she could trick him again.

"I'd be happy in a condo."

"Very well."

Nanna directed them to the yellow stucco building and into an elevator in a quietly elegant lobby with a marble floor and a modern crystal chandelier. "Not letting us stay on the first floor?" he asked.

As Nanna pressed the button that started the car moving, she gave him a curious look. "You can stay on the first floor." The elevator stopped and the doors opened onto a wide hall showcasing doors to four separate condos. "But I'm giving our guest a room with a view." She turned to Morgan. "It's a peaceful, panoramic view of the vineyard."

Morgan said, "Thank you."

But Riccardo got a funny feeling in his stomach. He shouldn't feel odd that his nanna wasn't

putting them on the same floor. They'd had separate rooms while driving across the US. They
weren't romantically involved. They weren't even
friends. In Nanna's mind, there was no reason
to keep them together. Especially given that his
grandmother didn't know Morgan had tried to
lose him in Vegas. All she was doing was giving
their "guest" the room with the best view.

But he got a weird, itching sensation along his
skin, thinking of her on one floor and him on
another.

Nanna punched in a code and opened the door
to the first condo. Like a proud owner, she offered
Morgan entry. "Everything's compact. Two bedrooms, two baths." She pointed to the right. "Sitting room." And to the left. "Kitchen."

Morgan glanced around appreciatively. "It's
lovely."

Riccardo agreed. The place was exceptional.
The duplex had been built in a rush and had
simple, plain architecture. The condos had been
lovingly designed with arches, rich hardwoods,
Carrera marble and wrought-iron accents.

The driver arrived with their bags. Morgan took

hers with a smile. "It's kind of light. I can carry it to the bedroom myself."

Nanna nodded her approval. "Come on, Riccardo. Let's get you to your room." She addressed the driver. "His bag is going to the first floor."

"Actually, I'd like to stay up here. On the second floor."

The driver stopped. Nanna frowned. "Here?"

"Well, there's no need to have people on two floors." Riccardo suddenly felt young and clumsy. He couldn't tell his grandmother Morgan had already tried to escape once. At least not in front of Morgan. "It's a safety thing."

Nanna laughed. "We're in the middle of Northern Spain's beautiful rolling hills. We don't even have a neighbor for miles."

"What if there's a fire?"

"Alarms will go off." Nanna sighed. "But there's no reason why you can't stay on the second floor. So, fine. I'll put you in the suite next door." She consulted a small blue book she pulled from her skirt pocket. "I have the codes for all the suites. Let's go."

Morgan stopped them. "Give me twenty minutes to shower and put on clean clothes, and I'll be ready to go shopping."

"Great. Meet me downstairs. I'll have the limo wait while I freshen up, too."

"Sounds good."

Nanna directed Riccardo out of Morgan's condo. "I think your dad and Santiago want to talk to you."

About Colonel Monroe, no doubt. Though Ochoa Online wasn't part of their business, they were protective of it, and they'd want to know what was going on. But that might be good. It wouldn't hurt to try different explanations on them so that when Mitch arrived Riccardo would know which one worked. Particularly since Morgan would be spending the rest of the day occupied—and sort of guarded—by his grandmother.

In the hall, Nanna gave him the code for the lock to his suite. He took his bag from the driver, using the same explanation Morgan had—it was light enough he could handle it. The driver left, but before Nanna could follow him, he caught her arm.

"Don't forget that Ms. Monroe is a runaway."

"Runaway *bride*."

"No, just plain runaway. She gave me the slip once in Vegas. Her dad is leaving for Stockholm next week, and she says she's going home then, but until she's safely on a plane back to the States, she's my responsibility. I brought her here to see how a family works. But also, so that you can talk to her. Help her sort out her feelings, figure out how to deal with her demanding dad."

"It would be my honor."

"Great." He loved his nanna's enthusiasm, but he also wanted to be clear about Morgan. "But I don't want her running again. Don't let her out of your sight today."

Nanna pointed a finger at him. "Shame on you for thinking she'd run."

"I don't know her well enough to *think* anything. I do *know* that she fooled me once. I'm not getting so comfortable with her that she does it again."

"Fine."

"Thank you."

Inside his condo, he showered and put on a clean pair of jeans and clean T-shirt. He tagged his dirty clothes for laundry, glad he had a tux and a few suits at his parents' house.

Clean and refreshed, he left his condo at the same time Morgan did. As she closed her door, she said, "Hey! Are you coming shopping with your nanna and me?"

His gaze cruised from her sandals to the top of her head. She wore shorts and a tank top, appropriate for the still-warm September weather, and though she'd clearly combed her thick yellow hair, it fell about her in wild waves.

He sucked in a breath, reminding himself she was the daughter of a client and a woman in emotional trouble, but he still wanted to tease and flirt with her, and that was worse for his sanity than the threat that she might bolt.

"Uncle Santiago wants to see me. My dad will be there, too."

"That's right. I remember your nanna saying that." She winced. "Sorry they're going to grill you about me."

"I'm not sure they are." He directed her to walk to the elevator. "But even if they do, I can handle it." He pressed the down button. "Besides, they might want to talk about their investments. They aren't part of Ochoa Online, but I handle most of the family's money."

"That's right. You're the moneyman." She smiled. "Probably the most important person in any business."

The elevator arrived. He shook his head as he motioned for her to enter. "My ego isn't delicate. You don't have to coddle me—" *or try to compliment me into trusting you* "—because I don't own Ochoa Online."

"I'm not coddling you. I'm an accountant, remember? I know how important your job is."

He said, "I remember," but confusion rolled through him. He'd been so suspicious of her, then attracted to her, then suspicious again, that he'd barely thought of her as a worker in her dad's company, a certified public accountant. But just then, when she'd reminded him she was an accountant, he saw a glimpse of the woman he'd found happily giving the stock seminar beside the slot machines. The supersmart CPA in glasses and gray canvas tennis shoes. Not the confused runaway bride. It was weird—

No. It was Morgan. The real Morgan. Honest. Honorable. With a warm smile and a big heart.

And *that's* why he'd wanted to kiss her. In the few days they'd had in the car, she'd gone from being confused to being herself.

And he liked her. Who wouldn't? She was a likeable person.

The elevator door opened. She exited first and he followed her out, his gaze unwittingly sliding from her shoulders to her butt. Her perfect butt. She was warm, funny, intelligent and sexy—

What the hell was wrong with him?

She was as forbidden to him as a person could be. Not only the daughter of a client, but also a woman who needed him. The absolute wrong kind of person for him to be interested in. Yet, he couldn't seem to stop himself from noticing everything about her.

They reached the door and he opened it for her. "Enjoy shopping with Nanna."

She smiled at him. "I will."

She all but raced up the cobblestone walkway to the limo, where his Nanna awaited her. "I hope I look okay."

Nanna kissed her cheek. "We'll get you an outfit at the first store. Maybe a cute dress with a big sun hat. Something chic and European," she said, holding the limo door open. "Then we'll have lunch. After that we can purchase the rest of what you need."

What Morgan said was lost as she entered the limo, but only an idiot would have missed the happiness in her voice. And *that* was what he wanted. Morgan to see real life with his happy, always fun grandmother, so she'd know what she was missing and be able to explain the future she wanted to her dad.

Once she got a dose of Nanna, she wouldn't want to run. She'd want to learn as much as she could. If there was one thing he'd realized about Morgan, it was that she was curious about what she'd missed. As long as Nanna was helping her figure things out, she'd happily stay with her. There was no reason to worry that she'd try to escape. Just as he'd planned, he could keep his distance from her.

He crossed the driveway between the cobble-stone path and the huge Ochoa Vineyards mansion and shook his head, wondering why that realization hadn't gotten rid of the odd feeling in his stomach.

Morgan was a good person, trying to figure out

her life before she had to talk to her domineering dad. She wasn't going to betray him. He shouldn't have this emptiness in his gut as if…

He turned the feeling around in his head, trying to figure it out. When the answer came, he squeezed his eyes shut.

As if…he missed her.

Damn it! That's what the weird, itchy feeling was about. He didn't mistrust Morgan. He felt odd about being away from her because he didn't want to be away from her. They'd spent almost every minute of the last few days together and he had grown to like her. That's why it felt so odd that his grandmother was separating them. Why watching her drive off had seemed wrong.

He missed her.

Damn it!

If he didn't watch out, she'd be his second Cicely.

He absolutely had to stay away from her.

He entered the first floor of the mansion, walking past the gift shop and down the long hall that led to his Uncle Santiago's office. With every step he took, his trepidation grew. He had done the right thing for Morgan, but his uncle and his dad would be more concerned with the Ochoa family than Morgan's situation with her dad.

He took a long breath, reminding himself that that was why he was going to Uncle Santiago's office. To convince his uncle and father that bringing Morgan to Ochoa Vineyards was the right thing to do, and that he could handle Colonel Monroe.

If he couldn't convince them, he'd never convince Mitch.

He opened the door and Santiago rose from behind the big mahogany desk. A tall, trim man with black hair and serious dark eyes, the CEO of Ochoa Vineyards could be intimidating.

"Uncle Santiago."

"Riccardo. Good to see you."

Seated on a chair in front of the desk, Riccardo's dad—Carlos, a younger version of Santiago—also rose.

"Riccardo!" He hugged his son. "Welcome home!"

Motioning for Riccardo to sit, his Uncle Santiago cut right to the chase. "We heard you brought a guest."

Riccardo sat on the chair beside his dad's. "Yes.

Morgan Monroe. I think she could benefit from some time with Nanna."

Santiago frowned. "With Nanna?"

"Morgan ran from her wedding. It's a long, complicated story, but when she really opened up about her dad, I knew I was in over my head. I figured Nanna could help sort this out."

Riccardo's dad said, "Ah."

Santiago sat back in his chair. "Nanna's good with people."

"Exactly."

The room got weirdly quiet. The conversation wasn't over by a long shot, but nobody said anything.

Finally, Santiago drew a slow breath. "You know that we're on the cusp of harvest?"

"Yes, and I'm glad to be here. Happy to help."

Carlos glanced at Santiago, then at his son. "We understand what happened with Morgan. She's got a powerful father. And we all know how difficult powerful men can be to live with."

Because his father was one of those men, Riccardo had to hold back a smile. "But?"

"We're at the most critical time of our year. This is Alonzo's first year of being in charge of the harvest. He'll choose the time we pick the grapes."

"And I think he's earned the right," Riccardo said.

"We do, too, or we wouldn't have given him such an important responsibility." Santiago sat back in his chair. "Our problem is that your guest comes with trouble at a time when we don't need trouble."

"She's fine."

"When her dad figures out where she is, he will most likely send someone after her."

"He already sent somebody after her. Me."

His father held his gaze. "And you failed him. Now he will send somebody else."

He looked from his dad to Santiago. "Are you saying that you want us to leave?"

"No. We want you to watch her. Every second of every day."

Riccardo's dad agreed. "Nanna is a wonderful person for her to talk to, but she's nobody's bodyguard."

Riccardo looked from his dad to his uncle. "First, I don't think Morgan's dad is going to figure out where we are. We ditched our phones. Got rid of the rental car in an obscure city. Flew here on a private plane."

Santiago frowned. "You don't think he'll figure out that you'd bring her to your family for protection?"

"He might. But this is a guy who worries what people think. He doesn't want any more bad publicity. The canceled wedding was disaster enough. Sending a contingent to Spain or even flying here himself would cause a stir. He's not going to give the press a chance at another story. He'll keep a lid on this. Which works in Morgan's favor. He won't do anything to make any waves. And that gives her the time she needs to decide what to say when she does go home."

Santiago rose, dismissing him. "Okay. We'll trust you on this. If it's peace and quiet she wants, we have it in abundance. If it's something fun and interesting to do, she can help harvest grapes. But I warn you. If she's using us to insult a former diplomat or make some sort of public spectacle, we will not be pleased."

He rose. "Morgan's not like that." He'd been with her in a silent car for days, listening to her story in bits and pieces the few times she'd talked.

At no point had she ever behaved like someone who wanted to hurt her dad—

But what if all that good behavior had been a ploy?

No. He didn't for one second believe it. She would not hurt her dad. She loved him.

"I saw genuine emotion in her eyes when she spoke of her dad cutting her out of his life. She does not want to lose him. She *does* want to be in the right frame of mind when she talks to him so that she can effectively argue her case."

That he'd seen in her eyes every time he looked at her. He'd heard it in her voice every time he'd talked to her.

His father sighed. "Yes, Riccardo, but if you're wrong, you won't be the only one to suffer. The family could be drawn into something that could end up an international scandal."

He hadn't thought of that. Or the impact on his family. He'd only seen his attraction, his fear of getting involved and Morgan's need for somewhere to stay until her dad left for Stockholm.

"I'll handle it."

"When she's not with Nanna, you must be with her."

"If that's what you want, that's what I'll do."

He walked out of the office. When the door closed behind him, he blew his breath out on a long sigh. For as much as he didn't want to tempt fate, he was going to have to stick to his runaway bride like glue.

CHAPTER SIX

DINNER WAS AT seven with cocktails at six thirty. Riccardo stopped at Morgan's condo at twenty past six. He knocked twice and she opened the door.

"Ready?" His gaze involuntarily rippled from her blond hair, which she'd pulled into a curly ponytail with a sunny yellow flower, to her blue strapless sundress, down her bare legs to white sandals. "Wow. You look amazing."

She fastened a slim bracelet on her wrist, calling attention to the porcelain skin of her bare arms, but also reminding him of how beautiful she was. She'd been cute, sweet, pretty, in blue jeans and T-shirts. But dressed up? With makeup? And all that gorgeous hair? She was a knockout.

"Once Nanna filled me in on how many family dinners we'd be having, my shopping list doubled."

He laughed, but the collar of his white shirt suddenly felt tight. The air-conditioned condo heated. He was back to being an up-close-and-personal bodyguard, and back to being face-to-face with his attraction.

"I couldn't very well wear that shiny black minidress to any of your nanna's dinners."

The heat in the room intensified. That little black dress had molded to her curves like a second skin—

He sucked in a breath and told himself to remember the conversation with his dad and Santiago. Morgan Monroe was potential trouble to his family. But more than that, she was vulnerable, like Cicely. Any feelings Morgan got for him could be nothing more than appreciation. He'd never again get involved with a woman who needed him. That was part of how he stayed happily single. No entanglements. No messes.

"And by the way, I intend to pay you back for every cent I charged to your card."

"That won't be necessary. I told you. We can expense it."

She caught his gaze. Her eyes held a tinge of something he couldn't quite interpret. "I want to pay you back."

That was so unexpected that for a second he almost lost himself in her beautiful blue eyes. But he caught himself. *No entanglements. No messes.* That was how a smart man stayed out of trouble.

She led him to her condo door and headed to the elevator as if she'd been in this building a million times. It wasn't until they were outside, on the cobblestone walkway, that he realized the last thing either one of them had said was about her insistence on paying him back.

He might not be allowed to be attracted to her, but he also wouldn't be rude. He forced himself to think of something neutral to say. "So, you're comfortable?"

"Yes. You have a beautiful estate."

"Technically, all this property belongs to the main house. My home, the house I grew up in—" he turned and pointed behind them "—is back there."

"I know." She smiled, her blue eyes lighting up when she caught his gaze, and everything inside him shimmied. When she was happy, there was no one prettier. "On the way back from shopping, Nanna had the limo stop so I could see the second vineyard. I met your mom. We had tea in the lovely backyard that fronts all those rows of grapes."

His spine stiffened. "You met my mother?"

"It would have been impolite to take the tour of the second vineyard and not go to the house to say hello."

Yes. It would have. The insulted feeling rumbling through him was ridiculous. Why should he care that Morgan had met his mother, that he didn't get to introduce them? It had been kind of Nanna to show her around, have her meet some of the people she'd be dining with tonight.

Everything was fine.

They walked up to the front entry of the mansion, then through the echoing foyer, past the gift shop and corridor that led to the vineyard offices and up the wide, circular stairway.

"This house is fabulous. It's hard to believe it's centuries old."

"Good maintenance."

"To be able to keep it this nice, I'm guessing your family never went through hard times."

At the top of the stairs, he motioned for her to walk down the hall. "Every family goes through hard times. Every business goes through hard times."

She stopped walking. "You just separated family and business."

"So? Though Ochoa Vineyards is the main client of Ochoa Online, they are two different companies. And I work for Ochoa Online. Not the vineyard. I'm more involved with my family than their vineyard."

"That's not how Nanna sees it. Everything's one big tangled vine to her. She never separates family and business."

He thought about that for a second, about why it would be significant to Morgan. "Your father doesn't separate family and business, does he?"

"No." She smiled at him. "And that's why I think Nanna was the perfect person for me to talk to. Our situations are the same. Technically, we both live at our jobs. She gave me a wonderful new perspective and a few inventive ways to approach my dad. Especially now that I have a plan for how to talk to him and Charles separately."

Relief rippled through him. His nanna had done exactly what he wanted. Morgan looked and spoke stronger than ever.

The sense that this was the real Morgan struck him again. She'd grown up a bit after running from her wedding. She'd also faced her demons— or at least had a plan to face them. She'd definitely changed some, but she was balancing out now, and this was her new normal. Stronger than she had been. Wiser than she had been. But her real self.

He looked over at her.

She smiled.

And the oddest sensation fluttered through him. He almost wasn't sure how to relate to the real her.

Calling himself all kinds of crazy, he pushed the buzzer that announced them and opened the door before he led Morgan through a small foyer and into the sitting room. Everyone in his family except Mitch and Lila sat on one of the tufted chairs or milled near the bar.

Spotting Morgan, Nanna broke away from a conversation with Santiago and his wife, Marguerite.

She caught Morgan's hands. "Darling. Thank you for the lovely day." She kissed both her cheeks.

"And if you don't take that sun hat with you when you leave Spain, it's mine."

"It's yours. There aren't many functions where I'd wear it," Morgan said with a sigh. Then she laughed. "Unless I go to the Kentucky Derby in the spring."

Nanna slid her hand beneath Morgan's arm and directed her away. "Have you ever been?"

"No. My father's not a horseman. I think he's crazy, though. We have acres and acres of land that aren't planted. We could easily put in a stable."

"So, you ride?"

"I love to ride!"

Her voice drifted off and Riccardo realized he was standing in the doorway like an idiot, watching her as if transfixed. He'd think it crazy, except she did look really pretty and it was fun to see that the confused woman he'd found in Vegas wasn't so confused anymore.

He walked to the bar.

Mixing drinks behind the polished wood, Alonzo said, "What can I get you?"

"A beer."

"Coming right up." Riccardo's tall, dark-haired

cousin pulled a bottle from a small refrigerator, opened the lid and handed it to him with a glass.

Alonzo's wife, Julia, sauntered over. Looking stunning in a pink dress, with her yellow hair pinned above her ears, Julia was the picture of a wealthy man's wife.

She caught Riccardo by the shoulders, stood on tiptoes and kissed his cheek. "I feel like I just saw you."

He laughed. "Mitch's wedding was only a few weeks ago."

"It's nice to have you around for more than holidays."

He said, "It's nice to be here." But Morgan's laugh floated to him. He automatically glanced around until he saw her, sitting on a sofa, Nanna on one side, laughing. Lila's mom, Francine, on the other.

He angled his thumb toward them. "I should go over."

Julia frowned. "Why? Nanna's entertaining her. Besides Francine seems happy to have another American around. We should let them chat."

Not wanting to make a scene, he smiled graciously. "Of course."

"Plus, you haven't said hello to your mother yet." Julia took his arm and turned him in the direction of his parents. "Go."

He walked to the corner where his parents and Mitch's parents chatted. His mother caught him in a huge hug. "Riccardo!"

"I heard you met Morgan today."

His mother's dark eyes lit up. Like Marguerite, she had a pinch of gray in her black hair, but only enough to add interest. Her simple dress was the color of a summer sky.

"Such a lovely girl. And such an odd story about her wedding. Her dad sounds like a tyrant." Then she frowned. "Why did you agree to help him?"

"I thought I was doing a good deed. Plus, he's a client."

His mother sighed. "Always a client."

His dad chuckled. "The boys are making an honest living, Paloma. Never discourage a child who knows how to make his own money."

Even though his dad's words were positive, when he caught his gaze Riccardo saw the warning in his father's eyes. Neither his dad nor Santiago would say anything to embarrass Morgan, but they didn't want any problems. It was his job to make sure there were none.

He said, "Right," as his gaze involuntarily drifted to the woman in his charge. Helping Morgan could ruin a big chunk of Ochoa Online or bring trouble to Ochoa Vineyards in the middle of harvest. But it wasn't because of Morgan. It was because of her dad. She was innocently beautiful, laughing with his grandmother. Her dad was the tyrant.

By the time he glanced back, his parents' conversation had changed from Riccardo to a possible trip to Greece in the winter. His mom was a yes. She loved Greece. Marguerite was intrigued. His dad wanted to see China and Santiago thought it was time they went to America. Miami Beach or maybe Vegas.

Alonzo took his arm and pulled him aside. "Come over here," he said. "Talk to the people who aren't semiretired and always planning their next trip."

Riccardo laughed, but Francine's louder laugh burst through the room, along with Nanna's and Morgan's. Whatever they were talking about, Morgan was having fun.

He'd loved the times she'd laughed with him. Loved the sound. Loved the way her eyes lit up. If she were anybody else, he would be wooing her with flowers and wine, late dinners, long nights in bed—

He cleared his throat to bring himself back to the present. Not only were thoughts like that wrong—he'd vowed he wouldn't romance another woman on the rebound—but they would also drive him crazy.

Alonzo began a discussion of this year's grape crop and Riccardo was grateful for the easy topic. Soon the staff announced dinner and they all walked to the dining room, where Nanna sat at the head of her table. His parents sat to Nanna's left and Mitch's parents sat to the right. Francine sat next to Mitch's parents, with Alonzo and Julia filling in beside them. Riccardo pulled out the chair beside his mother for Morgan and sat beside her.

As salads were served, Nanna directed the conversation to Alonzo and the new responsibilities he'd been assigned this year. Proud, he began sharing his plans, including the desire to buy the neighboring vineyard.

Everyone expressed approval.

Riccardo glanced at Morgan, who was staring at the dish in front of her.

"I see you finally got a proper salad."

She turned to him with a smile, her eyes bright and filled with laughter. "Yes. Thank goodness. It's lucky I tossed my wedding gown in the trash can of an airport bathroom. That turkey will never fit again."

He loved her American way of looking at things. Loved that she'd called her gown a big bird. Loved that she hadn't lost the odd sense of humor that had developed when she realized she'd never again fully be the old Morgan Monroe.

But telling her that would be too intimate, so he said, "American women want to be too thin."

She laughed. "Do you think you'd like a chubby version of me?"

He didn't think she was flirting, fishing for a compliment. She only said what was on her mind. He wanted to tell her he would probably like her no matter what size she was, but though he might have said that in the car, trying to help her get her thoughts straight, he couldn't have that kind of conversation with her now. Their discussions for the next few days would have to be surface, superficial.

Disappointment filled him, but he quickly shook his head to clear it. What was wrong with him? He should be glad his one-on-one time with Morgan was done. He'd already had to berate himself for missing her when she went shopping with Nanna. He could not let them get close again.

Before he got the chance to say anything, Nanna directed the conversation to Morgan. She didn't mind talking about her famous dad, making Riccardo's family laugh with her misadventures as his hostess, or her years at boarding school in New England. Julia interjected a few stories about her boarding-school experience and Alonzo joined in.

When they retired in the sitting room for after-dinner drinks, Morgan huddled in with Julia, talking about friends and silly things they'd done as kids. Though Morgan had been told the story of Julia stealing Alonzo from Mitch, she never gave any indication that she knew. Riccardo's dad continued the discussion of the neighboring vineyard that might come up for sale and suddenly it was almost midnight.

Morgan yawned. "Oh, my goodness. I didn't realize how late it was getting." She rose. "I think I'd best get myself to bed."

Riccardo set down his drink. "I'll walk you over."

"There's no need," Morgan said with a smile. "I'll use the time to unwind. It's a beautiful night."

"I insist."

Nanna frowned at him, but he got an obvious nod of approval from his father and Santiago.

When they were outside, under the star-filled sky, she said, "It was nice of your uncle and dad to want to make sure I got back to the condo safely."

Because she wasn't looking at him, he rolled his eyes. The old coots were afraid she'd run and bring the wrath of her father down on them at harvest time. But she didn't need to know that.

"They want all guests on the estate to be treated well."

"In spite of your scandals, your family is very nice."

"We're just normal people." He knew he wasn't supposed to get into any deep, thoughtful conversations with her, but this was something she needed to hear. "Every family has things happen. The trick is to forgive and move on."

"Yeah, well, it remains to be seen if my dad agrees."

He winced and said, "He will," but he let the conversation die. He already loved her laugh, missed talking to her and was seeing the real her, but he couldn't—wouldn't—get involved with another woman who needed him.

They reached the building, walked beneath the crystal chandelier in the lobby and into the elevator. The ride was short. In less than a minute, they were stepping into the corridor facing the doors to their condos. She walked to hers. He walked to his.

As she punched her security code into the keypad, she said, "I'm so confused about the time zones that I'm not even sure how long I've been up."

She pressed the final button and opened the door, but before she could go into her room, he said, "Technically, the nap we took on the plane counts as last night's sleep."

"Yes. I wouldn't have been able to keep up with

Nanna if we hadn't slept. And I'd have lost out on a great chance to see the light."

"The light?"

She shrugged. "You know…the way. The path."

He laughed. "What *did* you talk about with Nanna today?"

"My wedding. She asked about it. So, I told her."

"You told her everything?"

"Yes. Riccardo—" Her voice softened and her eyes became liquid pools of blue. "After talking to your grandmother, I understand why you brought me here and I really, really appreciate it."

He might not get involved with women on the rebound, but there was no denying that he liked Morgan. Especially her honesty. He didn't get a lot of that in the superficial dating life he'd created for himself, and for the first time he realized how much he missed true intimacy.

When he didn't say anything, she caught his gaze. "Maybe we're both tired?"

He had to be. Otherwise, he wouldn't be standing by yet another door with Morgan, wishing he could kiss her. Wishing he could comb his fingers through the thick strands of her hair. Wishing he didn't have to walk away.

But he did. She might be the most honest woman he'd ever met, but she was about a week out of a serious relationship. Plus, he was still her keeper, still responsible for her to her father. If the Colonel didn't like the idea of Riccardo not bringing her home, he'd probably explode if he thought the man he'd chosen to protect her wanted to seduce her.

He took another step back. "Good night."

She smiled. "Good night."

Everything inside him responded to that smile. The urge to kiss her rose, swift and urgent, a blinding need as sweet as it was desperate.

He forced himself to turn, to walk across the corridor and into his own condo.

CHAPTER SEVEN

A KNOCK AWAKENED Morgan the next morning. She grabbed her new pink satin robe and ran into the main living area of her condo. "I'm coming!"

Though it was foolish, she wished it was Riccardo. From the second he'd turned from his door and sauntered over to her the night before, her stomach had been in knots. Her chest had tightened. Her breaths felt shivery. He hadn't seemed to be able to pull himself away from her, and she was absolutely positive he was going to kiss her.

Just the thought had been delicious. Scary, yet wanted. Her throat got so tight, she'd have paid every cent in her trust fund to swallow—

But for the second time, he hadn't kissed her. He'd gone into his condo, leaving her with no choice but to enter hers, and the disappointment had been like an ache in her chest.

She'd tried to prevent her mind from jumping to the logical conclusion, but that was like telling her brain not to think of the color blue. The realization popped into her head like a neon light.

She liked him.

Not the way she'd liked Charles, the convenient, easy man who was always around. She liked Riccardo the way a woman was attracted to a man. A man who made her pulse skip and her insides quiver.

And he liked her, too. Enough to almost kiss her twice.

But when she answered the door, Nanna stood in front of a smiling man who pushed a cart with a tray of buttery croissants, a large bowl of fruit and a pot of coffee.

"I normally drink tea," Nanna said, motioning for the tall man to bring in the cart. "But for you and Lila, I'm more than happy to join you with coffee."

"That's very sweet," Morgan said, tightening the sash on her robe, fighting misery that made no sense. Even though it had been hard for Riccardo to walk away the night before, he *had* walked away. Maybe because he didn't want to get involved with the daughter of one of his biggest clients? Maybe because he still saw himself as being responsible for her?

And that seemed wrong. Now that she had her bearings, she could as easily spend the time before her dad's trip to Stockholm in Paris, and Riccardo would be off the hook. He did not need to be her keeper anymore. She was fine. She could leave.

Of course, if she left, she probably wouldn't see Riccardo again. If something didn't happen here in Spain, whatever was going on between them would be nothing but a few thoughts, a few almost kisses, a few nice conversations, easily forgotten when he got back to his real life in New York City.

"Are you okay, dear?"

Morgan's head snapped up. "Yes. Yes. I'm fine. I was just thinking about when I go home."

"Oh, honey. Of course you are."

The gentleman with Nanna slid the cart beside the table that sat between the kitchen and the arrangement of the sofa and club chairs that formed the sitting area. Nanna thanked him in Spanish and he left.

Morgan's training immediately kicked in and she said, "Please. Have a seat."

Nanna sat at the far end of the table. "Thank you." She frowned. "Are you thinking about going home because you're still afraid of talking to your dad?"

"No. Thanks to you, I have that all sorted out now," Morgan said, as Nanna took a croissant and offered the plate to her.

The knife Nanna had picked up to butter her croissant stopped. "Then what?"

She didn't think it appropriate to tell Nanna that just thinking about kissing her grandson made her shiver. So she said the first thing that popped into her mind.

"If I leave too soon I won't get to meet Lila and I'd love to talk to her."

"Why is that?"

"She grew up without her mom. Not the same way I did, but she still had to fend for herself, learn everything on her own. In all the thinking I've been doing since I ran from my wedding, I'm starting to wonder if I might have missed some things growing up without a woman to guide me."

"What do you think you've missed?"

"Well…" She thought about the crazy, wonderful feeling in her stomach the night before when she and Riccardo stood looking at each other, not speaking about much of anything, but not able to walk away. If she'd had normal teenage years, a mother to ask questions and dates with men her father hadn't chosen for her, she might have grabbed Riccardo's shirt collar, pulled him down to her level and kissed him.

But she couldn't tell his grandmother that.

Still, there were plenty of other things she'd missed out on. "Do you know I've never cooked beyond breakfast."

Nanna's face fell. "Seriously?"

"My last two years at university I had an apartment, but I really didn't prepare meals except eggs and toast, pancakes, French toast. My dad had made breakfasts for us when the cook had days off. I'd learned the basics watching him."

"And that's it? That's what you think you've missed?"

Embarrassed, she fumbled with her silverware. "That and a few other things that aren't easily explained. After hearing about Lila, it just seems talking to her would help me get a bunch of things straight in my own brain."

"She'll be home in a few days."

Morgan wasn't sure she had a few days. Her head said the smart thing to do would be to leave, get Riccardo off the hook and hope they met again. The crazy feeling in her stomach told her to stay. Spend enough time with Riccardo that he might call her when they returned to the States.

"In the meantime, I could give you a cooking lesson or two."

Morgan snapped back to reality. "I'm sorry. What?"

Nanna shot her a curious look. "I said I could give you a cooking lesson or two."

If Morgan's dad kicked her out and she ended up on her own, trust fund or not, she'd need to be able to cook more than eggs, but that hardly seemed like a reason to prolong her stay.

"Thanks, but…"

"I made these croissants."

Morgan looked at the flakey croissants that had melted in her mouth. Even if she decided to leave, she still had a day or two of planning to get herself off the estate. She could probably request the use of a limo and go to an airport without having booked a flight—she still had Riccardo's credit card to pay for a ticket—but that could mean hours waiting at the airport for the next flight to Paris.

And she couldn't get help from Riccardo or anyone in his family. If her dad found out they'd known where she was going, he'd blame Riccardo. So she had to leave on her own. To do that she had to get access to a computer.

"I'll show you my favorite websites to find recipes."

Her brain perked up. "Websites?"

"I do everything on the computer these days." She paused. "Actually, my tablet is much easier to keep on the counter while I'm cooking."

"You work from a tablet?"

Nanny smiled. "Yes. I might be old but I'm not crazy. Computers are better."

Maybe this was her answer to whether she should stay or go? If life was so easily going to give her access to the internet, maybe she was being nudged to leave.

"What time should I come to your residence?"

"First, we need to take a trip into town for your

gown fitting. Then we can come back here and make our own lunch."

"Here? In *this* condo? Not your kitchen?"

Nanna laughed. "The tablet's portable."

The relief of having access to the internet was briefly overshadowed by her hatred of deceiving Nanna, a smart woman who wouldn't be easily fooled for long. But she didn't want to give away her plan and risk making her dad angry with Nanna if he discovered she'd helped her. She had to act as if everything was fine.

"Sounds great."

They finished their breakfast and Nanna left to get ready for the trip to the seamstress. A household employee arrived a minute later to get the breakfast cart. Glad her father had insisted she learn four languages, she smiled at the middle-aged man.

"With whom do I speak about arranging for a car to take me somewhere?"

Stacking the dishes to make pushing the cart easier, he said, "Dial three-four-seven on the phone and you will be connected to household services."

That would get her off the vineyard to an airport. Now, all she had to do was get a ticket.

After the butler left, she showered and slid into a pretty blue dress and white sandals.

Happy, she picked up the big sun hat and sunglasses and walked out of her condo to meet Nanna for the dress fitting. As she pressed the elevator button, Riccardo's door opened.

She turned with a smile, but when she saw he wore only a white bath towel knotted around his waist, her mouth dropped open.

"Where are you going?"

He was male perfection. Broad shoulders, muscular legs, strong thighs and a flat stomach. Her heart thumped in her chest.

This was why she couldn't figure out what to do. She was absolutely getting feelings for Riccardo, and she believed he was getting feelings for her. Why else would he jump out of the shower to see her? But every time they got close, he pulled back. If she left now, he'd never contact her when they returned to the States.

Something had to happen between them. Something strong. Something important. So that he'd call her when they returned home—or she'd feel comfortable enough that she could call him.

"You're not going off the estate, are you?" He tightened his hold on the towel at his waist, taking her eyes to his flat stomach.

She had to clear her throat before she could answer. "I'm having my gown for the ball fitted this morning. Nanna's taking me."

"Oh, okay. Good."

Water drops clung to his wet hair and shoulders. He'd obviously raced out of the shower to catch her to find out where she was going...

She sighed. He still thought of himself as her keeper, thought of her as his responsibility.

The disappointment she'd been fighting all morning settled on her shoulders like a snow-covered coat. The silence in the little hall became deafening. He wasn't getting feelings for her the way she was for him. She was just another task on his to-do list.

She turned away and punched the elevator button again. The damn thing was taking forever.

"You look pretty in blue."

She closed her eyes and savored the compliment before she faced him again. "Thanks." She kept her voice light, friendly, though everything inside her wanted to walk over, place her hands on his gorgeous chest and kiss him. "You look very nice in your towel."

He laughed. "There's that sense of humor I've been missing."

She longed to bridge the space between them, to be close enough to touch him, close enough that she could flirt, but she stayed rooted to the spot. She had no idea what he felt for her. One minute he was silent, a man only interested in her because he was her keeper; the next he was telling her she was pretty. And she'd just officially broken off an engagement. It didn't seem right to be this attracted to another man so soon.

She was a mess.

Her whole life was a mess.

"You call it a sense of humor. I call it saying stupid things."

"To-may-to, to-maw-to." He smiled. That's when she noticed the morning stubble on his chin and cheeks. The sheen of desire in his dark, dark eyes.

Her heart felt like it did a cartwheel.

There was no point in trying to talk herself out

of this attraction. It was alive and well and scaring her silly.

"I'll see you later." Riccardo's eyes took another stroll down her blue dress and her bones felt like they melted.

"See you later." She turned and quickly got herself into the elevator, away from him. When the door closed, she pressed her hand to her chest. Freedom had multiplied the sensations running through her when he looked at her. Her pulse had scrambled. Her breath stalled. And all the while he'd smiled at her as if to say if she wanted him, really wanted him, she could have him, but she'd have to be the one to make the first move.

Where another woman might have reveled in the power of it, Morgan froze. He was sexy and strong, and she was just finding her feet. It would take years for her to catch up to him in confidence. Forget about ever having his swagger.

Plus, she was leaving. If not now, in a little over a week, when her dad went to Stockholm.

She closed her eyes, but she could still feel the warmth of his gaze on her. Curiosity about kissing him rose in her like a tsunami. The thought of leaving seemed so, so wrong.

Downstairs, she stepped outside, grateful the air was cool. Nanna stood by the limo, cell phone to her ear. When she saw Morgan, she waved as she said, "Yes, darling. I hear you loud and clear. Never out of my sight. Not for one second." She clicked off the call and smiled at Morgan. "We are ready?"

No. She wasn't ready at all. Freedom was airy and light and wonderful, but scary. Risky. At the same time, she didn't want to leave.

Still, was it fair to stay and keep Riccardo on the hook for her just because she was curious? She knew he'd been the person talking to Nanna. Making sure his grandmother watched her. He had to be tired of it.

The dress fitting took only an hour. Because Nanna had promised to teach her to cook, they returned to the vineyard to make lunch. Nanna went to her apartment to change clothes and Morgan slipped on a pair of her jeans and a big T-shirt.

Thirty minutes later, Nanna arrived with her tablet. "First we're going to make a dessert my friends call the better-than-sex dessert."

Morgan laughed. "Better than sex?"

Nanna tossed her a look. "Just trust me." She walked to the island counter. "It needs to be refrigerated before we can eat it, but that gives us time to make the paella."

Nanna pulled the dessert recipe up on her tablet, then placed a call to the kitchen to have everything they needed for the paella and the dessert delivered to Morgan's condo. When the ingredients arrived, they began cooking.

And it was easy. The condo was stocked with pots and pans, bowls and utensils, dishes and silverware. Everything required was at their fingertips or a phone call away to the staff, and following recipes was just like following instructions for chemistry experiments.

They ate the paella and dessert for lunch, and Morgan groaned with ecstasy. "That dessert is fabulous."

Nanna laughed. "I told you." She rose from the table. "Now it's time for my nap." She headed for the refrigerator. "But I'm taking the leftover dessert with me."

Dessert in hand, Nanna walked to the door. Morgan opened it for her. "I'll see you at supper."

Nanna stopped. "Oh, no, dear. I'm sorry. There

is no family dinner tonight. It's Saturday night. Everyone has plans."

"Plans?"

"Marguerite and Santiago are going out with friends. Riccardo's parents are having a private dinner at home. Alonzo and Julia are also staying in." She paused, caught Morgan's gaze. "I just assumed you would be doing something with Riccardo."

She almost told Nanna that Riccardo had said nothing to her, but stopped herself. Anybody who jumped out of the shower to ask where she was going wouldn't let her have supper alone.

She smiled at Nanna. "I'm sure we will."

Nanna kissed her cheek. "I'll see you tomorrow."

She closed the door and leaned against it, excitement bubbling through her. Tonight would be their first private dinner since they were on the road, when she'd looked like a street urchin. Tonight, she would dazzle him.

She spent an hour doing her toenails and fingernails, soaked in a bubble bath for another hour and then washed her hair. Dressed in pink silk pajamas, she was about to do her makeup when she had a flash of inspiration. She called the kitchen and had them bring up four different kinds of wine, and she slid them into the kitchen's wine cooler. She had no idea what Riccardo had planned, but no matter where they went for supper, even if it was only the family's restaurant, she could invite him into her condo for a glass of wine afterward.

She might be inexperienced but she wasn't dumb.

Eight o'clock that night, alone in her condo, wearing a sundress she hoped didn't scream "I've been waiting for you," with her hair fixed in a fancy style and her lips a striking shade of red, she was bored and miserable.

She paced the sitting room feeling like an idiot. She couldn't be angry with Riccardo for not showing up. He hadn't invited her to dinner. He hadn't even mentioned dinner. And she was an adult. He probably figured she could find her own food. On an estate with a restaurant, she should certainly be able to get something to eat.

She sucked in a breath. She wasn't hungry for food, but she did feel the need for comfort. A little sugar could go a long way right now. Especially if it came in the form of a better-than-sex dessert.

She was just about to call the kitchen to see if they had the recipe when she noticed Nanna hadn't taken her tablet. She hit a few keys and saw it hadn't been password-protected. She easily got in and opened the app that got her on the internet.

Her hand paused above the screen. Riccardo wasn't interested in her and she was about to make a fool of herself because she kept making ridiculous assumptions. Maybe it really was time to go.

Without further thought, she typed in the name of a popular airline and almost made reservations on the earliest flight to Paris—two days from now, but her fingers stopped again. It seemed dishonest to take off without telling Riccardo. Even with him ignoring her, she couldn't seem to deceive him.

She cleared the screen without making the reservation and looked up the recipe for the dessert. With her life back to being a confused mess, she wanted her pudding.

Though it was now long past eight, she called the kitchen. Speaking Spanish, she asked for the ingredients she needed to make the dessert. While she waited for them, she ducked into her bedroom, yanked off the dress, combed out her hair, wiped off the red lipstick, took out her contacts and threw on old jeans and a T-shirt.

She returned to the sitting room, sliding her big glasses on her nose just as there was a knock on her door. She opened it to find someone from the kitchen staff and the ingredients she'd asked for.

She refused to think about Riccardo as she pulled a glass baking pan and two big bowls out of the cupboards and went to work. The crust was first since it had to be cool before she could put the cream cheese filling on top. She mixed the butter, nuts and flour together, spread it out on the bottom of the baking dish and put it in the preheated oven.

Fifteen minutes later, the timer rang. Pot holder in hand, she pulled out the finished crust and beamed. Perfect. It was all so easy, she felt like a dolt for not cooking her entire life. And for caring what Riccardo thought. She would go home to a whole new life. A life where she wasn't just an equal with her dad, but she could cook. Take care of herself.

As the crust cooled, she gathered the cream cheese, whipped topping and vanilla extract and blended them using a hand mixer Nanna had shown her was in the cupboard. Relaxation filled her. She'd been told her mother had been an excellent cook and now she understood why she'd taken the time to prepare meals though they had a staff. Preparing food came with a wonderful sense of accomplishment.

With the wet ingredients blended, she opened the confectioner's sugar and measured a cup and a half, dumping it on top of the cream-cheese filling. She turned on the mixer and dipped the beaters into the powdered sugar and—*poof!*—she was covered in white dust.

It surprised her so much she screamed.

CHAPTER EIGHT

RICCARDO WAS JUST about to punch in his key code, when he heard Morgan scream. He raced to her door, damning his family for insisting on locks and steel doors he couldn't break down. He banged on the door, calling, "Morgan!" as he tried the knob. It gave—because she hadn't locked it—and he shoved open the door and raced inside, only to find Morgan standing by the counter covered in white powder.

He laughed.

She gave him an evil look. "What exactly do you think is so funny?"

"Oh, my gosh. You…" Another laugh escaped. Even the lenses of her big glasses were covered in white. "What were you doing?"

She took off her glasses, whipped a paper towel off the roll and cleaned the lenses. "I was cooking."

He sniffed the air. "Smells good."

"That's the crust of the dessert your grandmother taught me to make this afternoon."

"And you decided to make it again because you were bored?"

Her chin lifted. "No. I got hungry for it."

He pointed at the powder-covered countertop. "You should have gotten hungry for a sandwich."

Her chin rose a little higher, clueing him in that she was truly angry. And he supposed she had a right to be. The entire family had other plans that night. He'd expected to be out of his meeting with Alonzo in time to take her somewhere. But Alonzo kept talking about wanting the third vineyard, needing the house for himself and Julia, in spite of the fact that the seller had finally provided the purchase price and it was way over what the vineyard could afford to pay.

Meaning Riccardo had totally abandoned Morgan.

"I wanted dessert."

Not sure how to make amends, he took a paper towel and brushed off her shoulders. "Your back is comically clean."

"Ha. Ha."

"Oh, come on. Don't pout. It's very funny to see

somebody covered head to toe in white stuff in the front but perfectly clean in the back."

"Yeah. It's hysterical. I'm going to change."

"It might be a better idea to finish making your dessert first." Avoiding a glare, he glanced around. "How much more do you have to do?"

She sighed and walked back to the mixer. "I just have to beat this powdery stuff in, then make instant pudding."

"I could help."

She hesitated. He almost wished she'd tell him to go back to his room. It was too late for dinner. And damn if she wasn't adorable trying to be domestic.

"Maybe a little supervision isn't a bad idea." She eyed him skeptically. "Do you cook a lot?"

"Enough to know that you don't put mixer beaters into dry powder sugar and expect to stay clean."

He walked over to the counter and pulled a large spoon from a side drawer. He folded the white powder into the cream-cheese filling a few times, then said, "Okay, try it now."

She lowered the beaters and in under a minute it was blended. "I suppose I should thank you."

He leaned against the counter. "That would be nice."

She peeked over at him. "Thank you."

He looked into her pretty blue eyes and saw a combination of chagrin and desperation that made him long to hug her. But he remembered he didn't get emotionally involved with needy women or even nice women. He didn't do relationships. He had simple, uncomplicated flings. That was why his life was easy.

"You take all this too seriously, you know."

She picked up the bowl and began layering the cream-cheese filling onto the cooled crust. "All what?"

"Normal stuff. Things you think the rest of us know but you don't. Lots of it is common sense. And for the rest there's YouTube."

She looked over at him, studied him for a few seconds, then laughed. "YouTube?"

He shrugged. "Sure. Take that box of pudding mix. I'll bet if you Googled it, you could find a YouTube video on how to make it."

She presented the box to him. "Directions are right here."

"Sure. You had the directions for the white stuff, too, but you ended up covered in powder."

"Very funny."

"At least now you know you won't do that again."

She peered over at him. "No. I won't. I'm not that stupid."

"Actually, you're not stupid at all." He spotted the wine in the cooler and strode over to grab a bottle. He hadn't meant to leave her unattended through dinner. He owed her some company for a little while.

While she made the pudding, he found two glasses and poured rich red wine into them. "This is last year's. My dad thinks it's too sweet. I think it's perfect."

She took the glass, sampled the wine and smiled. "I like it."

She poured the pudding onto the layer of cream cheese then slid the pan into the refrigerator. "I'm guessing you're hanging around because you want some of that dessert."

He laughed. "Yes and no." Knowing it was time for the apology he should have made right away, he said, "I'm sorry I left you alone this evening."

She didn't accept his apology, but looked away. She might have thought that made it appear like she didn't care but it actually told him just how much she had cared.

"It takes an hour to be firm enough that we can cut it."

He lifted the bottle of wine. "We can kill time with this."

She shrugged. "Okay. Sure."

He headed for the French doors. "Have you used the deck yet?"

"Your nanna has kept me kind of busy."

"Then you're in luck. There's a full moon. You can see for miles."

Nerves rattled through Morgan. It wasn't the perfect evening she'd seen in her head, but he was here and he was staying for a while. Plus, hadn't she thought that morning that she could have him but that she'd have to make the first move? This might be the night she got the chance.

The air was warm and the sky was clear. A huge golden moon watched over the silent vineyards. A woman who'd just walked away from a wedding, broken up with a fiancé and learned to cook was alone on a deck with the first man who'd ever really attracted her.

Yeah. This was going to work.

She sat on one of two chaise lounges on the well-appointed deck. There was a round glass table in the corner that would be perfect for morning coffee and a small square table sat between the two chaises. Riccardo set the wine bottle there, as he lowered himself to one of the chaises.

"So Nanna tells me you know what you're going to say to your dad."

Tonight she didn't exactly want to talk about her dad, but the conversation had to start somewhere. This was as good of a place as any.

"I have a general idea, but it's not like I made a PowerPoint presentation with slides." She shook her head with a laugh. "Your grandmother thinks that I should go home, tell him I'm not happy with our relationship and then leave."

Riccardo peered over. "Leave?"

She ignored the feeling that zinged through her when she looked into his eyes. Especially since the expression in them seemed so neutral.

"She thinks that if I try to argue he'll best me. But if I take a stand and leave, but tell him where

I'm going—the address to my new apartment— ultimately he'll come to me willing to talk...or maybe listen."

He took a long breath, as if thinking through what she'd said. "That idea has some merit."

"But?"

"He's a busy guy." He glanced at her. "Men do things differently than women."

"No kidding." She was on pins and needles, thinking this might be her chance to make a move, and he was talking about her dad. Men certainly did do things differently than women.

"I'm serious. The man runs a huge business and he's still an advisor to more people than you and I even know. Heads of state come to him for advice all the time. What if you leave, one of his friends has a crisis and asks for help and he's tied up for weeks?"

The nervous torment of wondering how to make the first move disappeared. She silently held his gaze, not quite sure what he was telling her.

"You could be sitting in an apartment in New York City, waiting for a call that he's not even thinking about making because he's handling a crisis."

"You're saying I'm not that important to him?"

"No, I'm saying that people are creatures of habit. He's accustomed to solving problems. Accustomed to being called upon. To dropping everything to fix the world. And while he's doing that, you'd be sitting alone, thinking he doesn't care about you when really he's just busy."

She let all that slide around in her brain. It was the reality of their relationship. Not that her dad believed everything in the world was more important than she was. It was more that he was a statesman, a diplomat. It was his calling. If someone needed him, he went.

And she would be waiting for a phone call that wouldn't come.

She shook her head, jarring the picture of her sitting by a silent phone out of her brain because it was wrong. She was an adult. If she spent her time waiting by the phone for her dad to call? That was on her. Not him. She should be out having a life. *Her life.* Not being part of her dad's.

"Oh, my gosh."

"What?"

"You're right. Though Nanna got me thinking in the right direction, you just filled in the blanks.

I need to move out of my dad's house. But not because I don't want him to find me. Because I need my own life. I also need to get a job somewhere other than the vineyard." She finished the wine she'd been sipping in a quick swallow and refilled her glass.

"That's not what I said."

"It didn't need to be what you said. That's the conclusion I came to after thinking through what you said." She tapped his arm. "Come on, Riccardo. I'm twenty-five and I still live with my dad. I can't complain about him running my life when I'm not doing anything to run it myself."

Riccardo just stared at her. Had she just taken the advice he'd given her and twisted it to make his problem worse? If she told the Colonel he'd helped her decide to move out, the old man would forget everything he knew about diplomacy and shoot Riccardo first and ask questions later.

"You're getting ahead of yourself."

"I don't think so." She took a sip of wine, then rose from her chaise with a laugh. "Your nanna thought leaving was a way to make him realize that I was serious. But the truth is, the best way to make him realize that the way he sees me needs to change is for *me* to change."

She walked over to the railing. Moonlight spilled over her hair and gave her face a radiant glow. "I wasn't a spoiled child. From the time I was twelve, I was my dad's hostess and that wasn't easy. I never saw myself as dependent upon my dad. I saw us as a team. But I never realized that team was holding me back from becoming me." She took another sip of her wine. "I'm a CPA, for heaven's sake. I could change the world."

He took a long gulp of his wine, almost afraid to talk for fear of making things worse. In the end, he could only argue the obvious. "CPAs don't change the world."

"Oh, yeah?" She turned from the railing, her face radiant, her smile so bright it competed with the moonlight. "How do you know?"

"Because I'm a CPA and I haven't changed the world."

"Really? Look around you. You could have stayed in your parents' home, working a low-level job for this vineyard, cashing in on your family name. Instead, you left."

"Because there was nothing for me here."

She opened her arms, waving her wineglass out over the railing. "You just made my point. There is nothing for me at my dad's vineyard, except to be his employee and hostess. As both of those, I'm under his command. Out here in the world, I can be anything."

"You're a CPA."

"Exactly!"

Riccardo's head spun. He set his glass on the small table, rose from the chaise and walked over to her. "I meant, you can't be *anything*. You have to work within the parameters of your degree."

"I know that. I'm just thinking out loud. And we've already decided I'm not stupid."

He'd never thought she was. From the second he'd seen her giving the stock seminar behind the slot machines, he'd realized she was more than the woman portrayed in the press. More than a woman in trouble. He'd just never realized how perfect she was. How wonderful.

Her smile grew. She glanced out over the rows of harvested grapes. "Maybe I'll get a job here."

"What?" Wonderful or not, she couldn't stay here. If the Colonel thought he or Mitch helped her escape, he'd bring the full force of his power down on them.

"I know Ochoa Vineyards is fully staffed. I was talking about Spain. I'm fluent in Spanish, French and Italian and Mandarin. I love Europe." She began to pace. "I need to put together a résumé. Start looking at companies, seeing if there's anywhere I want to work. Any company looking for someone with my skills."

"Once again, I think you're getting ahead of yourself."

"I don't!" She set her glass on the round glass table, walked over to him. "I'm behind where I'm supposed to be. True, I got some experience working for my dad's companies, but my work was pretty much low-level stuff."

"Everybody starts at the bottom."

She considered that. "Okay. Good. Since I've already started at the bottom, what you're saying is that I need to find a next-level job."

Riccardo groaned. "I'm not saying anything. I'm not giving advice. I'm not making recommendations."

"I know. I don't need your advice. I've got this."

She stood on her tiptoes and pressed a quick kiss to his lips.

As if realizing what she'd done, she froze in place.

Their gazes caught.

Temptation roared through him. So swift and so strong, he didn't have time to combat it. She was sweet. She was funny. And she drew him in a way no woman ever had before.

His hands went to her shoulders, his head descended and his lips pressed to hers with the determination of a man taking what he'd wanted for what seemed like forever.

His lips slid across hers, tasting a hint of the sugar that had covered her face when he'd arrived, sending a bubble of laughter through him, causing him to take the kiss deeper, to open his mouth and encourage her to open hers. When she did, he plundered. She was like a rare treat, water to a thirsty man.

She rose to her tiptoes and gave as good as she got. As desperate as he was, she nestled against him and that's when warning bells began to chime.

Not because she was a woman who had just

gotten out of a relationship, but because of who he was. Right now, he could take anything he wanted from her and she'd let him.

And then he'd know real regret. Because he wasn't a man who settled down, not anymore. He was a man who had flings. If they did what he wanted to do right now, he'd walk away tomorrow morning without looking back, and he'd hurt her.

He broke the kiss and stepped back quickly. "Okay. That's the last time we're going to do that."

She blinked. Her big blue eyes seemed bigger, shinier. "Why?"

He walked over to the small table between the chaises, picked up his wine and downed it. "You may not understand this now, but you're not in any kind of condition to make the decisions you think you want to make."

"*I* think *I* want to make? There were two of us in that kiss."

"Okay, let's look at this purely from my vantage point. I got involved with a woman who was fresh off a relationship. We were together two years and when her old boyfriend came back, she dropped me. Even after all the time we dated, after accepting an engagement ring, planning our wedding, she'd never gotten over her ex."

She fell to the chaise beside him. "Wow."

"No matter how angry I wanted to be with her, I had to recognize that I was as much to blame as she was. She was emotionally vulnerable. I didn't think I'd taken advantage of that. But I sure as hell didn't give her time to heal." He shook his head. "No. I thought I could help her heal. But the real bottom line was she wasn't ready. And here you are a week after running from your wedding. You haven't even officially talked to Charles yet."

Her head came up. "Yes. I did. I called him."

His heart stumbled. "You did?"

She nodded. "I couldn't very well be looking at you in nothing but a towel when I hadn't settled things back home."

He laughed.

"You think that's funny? You think I want the feelings I have for you? I've fought them at every turn."

"Well, keep fighting them because this—" he motioned from him to her and back to himself again "—is wrong."

"I don't think so. I fought it and fought it and

fought it and what I feel keeps getting more and more real."

"Okay, then how about this. Getting dumped in such a public way, losing a woman I adored, changed *me*." He caught her gaze. "I decided relationships weren't for me and I learned how to have fun without getting involved. I could easily take what you're offering and walk away." He shook his head. "This time I wouldn't get the broken heart. You would."

He turned then, not giving her a chance to reply. He walked through her condo, to his own, where he closed the door, trying to make himself feel safe. Not from her. From himself. He'd never been so tempted by a woman before.

Then he realized his lips still tingled. He pressed two fingers to his mouth. *She'd kissed him.*

And he'd liked it. Really, really liked it. And not just sexually. Morgan was sweet and funny and smart. *Everything about her* called to him.

He pushed those thoughts out of his brain. She might find him attractive, she might be ready to move out of her dad's house, get another job, start another life, but only a week ago she'd been ready to marry another man.

What if she went home, and in the familiar surroundings of her life realized she'd made a mistake?

What if she went home, saw Charles and changed her mind?

The risk was too great.

With this being his second time of making the same mistake, the potential humiliation was off the charts.

He should stay away from her. But he couldn't. He had a father and uncle who wanted to make sure she wouldn't bring trouble to Ochoa Vineyards. Little did they know, she already had.

CHAPTER NINE

MORGAN WAS EATING a croissant from a basket sent over by Nanna the next morning when there was a knock at her door. Done with hoping it was Riccardo—because she'd made an idiot of herself the night before and she didn't want it to be him, she was surprised when she answered and found him on the threshold.

Wearing chinos and a white shirt, he looked like a businessman on casual Friday. Which, unfortunately, appealed to the CPA in her. Her heart tumbled. Memories of their kiss sent warmth through her. But she could not fall in love with him. As he'd said the night before, she wasn't emotionally ready. It shamed her that he'd had to spell it out for her. To remind her that she'd need time to heal from one relationship before she could start another. But she wouldn't let him see that. She'd embarrassed herself enough in front of him.

Glad she'd dressed in jeans and a T-shirt before coming out of her bedroom that morning, she smiled innocently, as if their conversation the night before hadn't happened. "What's up?"

"Today's an off day." He shrugged. "I thought I'd take you to town, buy you lunch."

"You're not in charge of my happiness." It made her feel weird to say it, but it was true. That was another lesson she'd learned after spending the entire day primping, fancying herself up, to see him—only to have him not show up when she thought he should. From here on out, she would stand on her own two feet. Think for herself. Protect herself. Entertain herself.

"I'm fine. I'll find something to do." She pointed to the kitchen island, where Nanna's tablet still sat. "Maybe I'll cook something."

He laughed. "No. I don't want you to be bored and I don't want you to leave Spain with negative feelings after our conversation last night. Let me show you around."

Because he asked, didn't order, she softened a little. He was right. She didn't want to go home with weird feelings about him. He'd given her the chance to think through her life when her dad wanted him to take her home. And they had gotten along well until she'd kissed him. It only seemed fair that she capitulate, go with him and give them both back the good feelings they'd had toward each other.

"Okay, give me ten minutes to dress."

His eyebrows rose. "Ten minutes?"

"Seriously. I'll just change into a sundress and slip into sandals."

"No makeup?"

"Are we meeting royalty?"

He laughed. "No."

She headed for her bedroom. "Then I'm fine."

"It's very warm. You should also bring that sun hat you bought with Nanna."

She stopped. It struck her as odd that he remembered an offhand conversation from dinner the first night she got there. Charles sometimes couldn't remember important things she told him. Riccardo even remembered insignificant details. It filled her heart with something indescribable, then she pushed that thought out of her head.

He wanted nothing to do with her.

And who could blame him? The woman who'd canceled *his* wedding had just left a relationship when she'd met him. It was either a terrible coincidence or a cosmic joke that they'd met right after her breaking up, but she understood.

Anything between them would be foolish.

She slipped into a pink sundress, found her sunglasses and snagged the big sun hat Nanna liked.

When she returned to the sitting room, he was staring out at the deck—where she'd kissed him the night before, then he'd kissed her.

Really kissed her.

Her breath wanted to stutter. She stopped it, suddenly realizing that it might be her own fault she was getting feelings for him. Every time something happened between them, she infused it with meaning. Maybe if she'd let herself see the real Riccardo, and stop making a big deal out of everything, these feelings would disappear?

He turned from the window. "You look great."

There. See? Here was her first realization. He was a man who complimented her. Because she wasn't accustomed to being complimented, she lapped up his praise as if it had more meaning than it did.

He was right. They needed an outing together. But not so they could remain friends, but so she'd see how badly she continually misinterpreted him.

"And I'm all ready to go."

They walked outside to a red Porsche that sat in front of the condo building. He opened the door for her—like a gentleman, nothing romantic about that at all—and she slid inside.

As he drove them into the small town where she'd shopped and lunched with Nanna, he pointed out various vineyards, and places he and Mitch had played as kids. In town, they walked along cobblestone streets fronting small businesses in buildings that looked a lot like gingerbread houses from fairy tales. He told her stories about the baker, the hardware store owner and the tavern owner, who was a friend of his, making her laugh enough to remind her that he was a nice guy. A friendly guy. And though that was good, it wasn't a reason to fall in love. He treated everybody well.

With the warm sun beating down on them, and the soothing tone of his voice washing over her, she began to feel normal again, except smarter. The sheep in her had died the day she ran away from her wedding. Her thoughts really had cleared in Spain and she had a plan for her life. True, Riccardo had helped her, but maybe it was best not to think about that. It brought all kinds of appreciation to the surface and made her like him again.

And she didn't want to like him. It was too soon. Her emotions were scrambled. The cautious part of old Morgan Monroe resurfaced and she let it. Casual Morgan did nothing but get her into trouble.

They decided on the bistro across from the park for lunch, sitting at a wrought-iron table with matching chairs. The town wasn't crowded, but tourists strolled the streets. As they finished eating, a mime took up residence at the edge of the park.

She pointed across the street. "Look at that."

"He's a regular."

"He's very good."

"Eh...he's so-so."

She gaped at him. "Really? So-so? Can you juggle three oranges?"

"Anyone can juggle three oranges."

Morgan held back a laugh. Finally, a flaw. The arrogance she'd seen in Vegas was back. And she couldn't resist teasing him.

"Do you want to go over and try?"

He gave her a funny look. "You don't believe me?"

Suddenly feeling a little crazy for pushing him, she batted her hand. "Never mind."

He shoved his chair back. "You don't believe me."

"It doesn't matter if I believe you or not."

He took her hand and forced her to stand. "Come on. No one calls Riccardo Ochoa a liar."

She couldn't help laughing as he all but dragged her across the quiet street.

When they reached the mime, he said, "Can I see those?"

The mime tilted his head in question as his face twisted in confusion, clearly getting his point across without saying a word.

Morgan pressed her hands to her chest to keep from hugging him. "You're so good!"

The mime bowed.

Riccardo sighed.

The mime bowed to him and handed over the three oranges. Riccardo took them and juggled them like an expert, even throwing one behind his back without missing a beat. The small crowd that had gathered applauded.

Done, he handed the oranges back to the mime then took her hand. "There. See. I can juggle."

She laughed and pointed behind him as the mime picked up a forth orange and began to juggle more oranges than Riccardo had. "I think you've just been bested."

He faced the mime. "Are you challenging me?"

The mime shrugged.

Laughing, Riccardo took the four oranges from his hands and juggled them with ease. But when he stopped, he didn't lay down the four oranges, he picked up a fifth.

Like a pro, he juggled the five oranges. The growing crowd cheered.

The mime took the five oranges from Riccardo and juggled them but not with the ease Riccardo had. When he stopped, he picked up a sixth orange. He barely managed to juggle all six, but he did it.

The crowd clapped.

Grinning, the mime handed the six oranges to Riccardo.

But Riccardo shook his head, then he bowed. With a laugh, he said, "You are the better juggler."

The mime strutted in a small circle. Riccardo applauded him, then dropped some money into the hat the mime had sitting on the ground for donations.

Walking back to the Porsche, Morgan said, "What did you just do?" She glanced back at the mime, then at Riccardo again. "You'd juggled the five oranges much better than the mime had. You'd have easily done six. Why'd you give up?"

He said nothing.

"Oh, my gosh! You lost on purpose!" The craziness of it caused her to stop walking.

He opened the car door for her.

She stared at him as she rolled the whole thing around in her brain. "You didn't want to embarrass him."

He pointed at the door and she scrambled over and got inside. He closed the door and rounded the car, getting in behind the steering wheel.

"Admit it." She almost added, *You lost on purpose because you saw how he bobbled the five oranges and didn't want to embarrass him.*

But when the truth of it sunk in, she closed

her mouth. He wouldn't want credit for that. She glanced at the mime, who was happily juggling his oranges, bowing when someone tossed money in his hat, and her heart swelled. She wasn't falling in love with Riccardo Ochoa because she was needy...or because she was on the rebound. He was a great guy. Unlike anybody she'd ever met. And very much like somebody she'd want in her life forever.

Riccardo walked her to her door, annoyed with himself for challenging the mime. It had been easy enough to get out of the contest when he saw the man wasn't as skilled as he was. But Morgan had seen right through it.

Because she was smart. And he *loved* that she was smart. The combination of beauty and brains just about had him mesmerized. But that was the problem. They weren't right for each other. She was a woman who'd just got out of a serious relationship, and he was a guy who had built protective walls because he'd been hurt by someone who'd just got out of a serious relationship.

He could not like her. He would hurt her. Or she would hurt him.

But even that line was blurring now, which meant he liked her a lot more than was advisable.

They stopped at her condo door. She punched in the key code. "Why don't you come in. It's four hours 'til dinner. There's plenty of time for us to have a glass of wine on the balcony."

He glanced outside at the place where they'd had wine the night before, where he'd helped her come to another conclusion and where she'd kissed him.

The power of that simple kiss snapped through him and he wanted nothing more than to kiss her again. To drink wine and laugh. Except that would only make him like her more. As it was, he was dangerously close to letting go, letting himself enjoy her company. Then, when she left, when she got home and realized how much she'd missed her life, he'd barely be a passing thought. And if he as much as moped one day over her, his family would think he was an idiot.

It was one thing to fall for one woman who'd been on the rebound. Falling for a second would make him the world's biggest fool.

Which was why he said, "No. Thanks. I'm going to look at some accounts before dinner."

She smiled. "Why don't we have the glass of wine, then I could come over to your condo and help you do whatever it is you have to do."

He laughed. "Right. I'm going to audit accounts after a couple of glasses of wine?"

"I said one glass."

"I saw how you are with wine. I saw you refill your glass twice last night without even hesitating."

"Because it was good."

The simplicity of her answer soothed his agitated soul. But that was what being with her did to him. Made him happy. Calmed him down. Made him feel like he'd found his place. Like he wasn't the one helping her. She was the one helping him. And in a way she was. He hadn't realized how empty his life had been without intimacy until he'd met her.

"Thanks." He longed to run his fingers through her hair, to be allowed to touch her. Just to have contact. But none of this was real for her. Oh, she might think it was, but being away from her dad, Charles, the gossip about her running from her wedding, had put her in something of a protective bubble. She'd be strong about some things when she returned home, but she would realize she missed others.

Maybe even Charles.

"How about if I help before the wine?"

He stepped back. "No. I'm good. We'll both have enough wine with dinner at Nanna's tonight."

She nodded, opened her condo door and walked inside.

He shoved his hands in his trouser pockets as his heart drooped. It was cruel of fate to find him a woman to bring him back to life after Cicely, to remind him of all the things he'd wanted, to long for things he'd thought were beyond his reach. Because Morgan wasn't any more able to give them to him than Cicely had been.

He turned and headed for his condo. He was thankful she only had a few more days before she could go home, but when he walked inside his quarters that odd feeling struck him again. The one he'd had the day they'd arrived in Spain...

That he missed her.

That his life just wasn't complete without her in it.

He knew what was happening. Despite his best efforts and all his good arguments, it would hurt when she left.

* * *

Morgan dressed in a peach floral sheath dress for dinner that evening. Nerves pricked at her stomach but she ignored them. She'd stood by her door after she'd gone inside that afternoon, waiting to hear Riccardo leave but he didn't. For a good five minutes, he stayed in the hallway, in front of her door.

She'd thought he would change his mind about the wine, thought he might actually be changing his mind about everything. God knew she was. Every time she tried to tell herself she wasn't in the right frame of mind to be making emotional decisions, he did something wonderful and she would know she wasn't falling for him because she was vulnerable. She was falling for him because he was a man worth loving.

She couldn't even think about him without losing her breath.

In the end, he'd walked away and gone to his condo to look at his accounts, but they were having dinner that night with the family. They would have five minutes alone walking over and five minutes walking home—then there would be time at her door. He might kiss her again. Or maybe she would kiss him…

Twenty minutes went by with her pacing in front of the sofa, waiting for him to knock on her door. When she recognized they'd be late if they didn't leave now, she wondered if he'd decided not to walk her over. He'd never actually said he'd get her for dinner, but it was common sense to go to family meals together. They were on the same floor of the same building. He couldn't, wouldn't, "ditch" her.

When another five minutes went by, she knew she either left now or she'd be late. Rationalizing that he could be on the phone with someone or napping, she realized that if she waited for him she'd look like an idiot who couldn't even walk herself next door.

She stepped into the hall and stood staring at Riccardo's door.

She could knock. If he answered, she could say something light and fun, like, "Hey, we're going to be late if you don't get a move on."

But knocking on his door seemed hopelessly desperate. She refused to be desperate. She might want to kiss him. She might even be falling in love. But Morgan Monroe was not desperate.

She raced along the cobblestone path and up the stairs to Nanna's. She did as Riccardo always did, pressed the doorbell, but walked inside without waiting for someone to answer.

She entered the sitting room with a smile. "Good evening, everyone."

A general greeting came from his family, as Nanna walked over and escorted her to the sofa. "Get her some wine, Alonzo."

Alonzo complied and brought her a nice glass of red. Taking a sip, she glanced around surreptitiously and didn't see Riccardo.

She wanted to ask. But what was the point? If he was on the phone with someone, no one at Nanna's would know. If he was napping, same deal.

Still, no one seemed concerned that he was late, and when dinner was served and he still wasn't there, no one mentioned it. No one mentioned him all night.

At the end of the evening, Julia rose from the sofa and said, "Time to get moving." She caught Alonzo's hand and pulled him from his seat before she turned to Morgan. "Riccardo asked us if we'd walk you home."

Her breath froze at the mention of his name until she realized what Julia had said. "He asked you to walk me home?"

"Yes," Alonzo said. "He had a long day, and said he was too tired to join us for dinner, but didn't want you walking home alone. Especially since our town house is on the way."

He wasn't at dinner because he'd had a long day?

She'd been with him most of the day and she wasn't tired—

Unless he just plain didn't want to see her?

He hadn't wanted to come to her balcony for wine, didn't want to have dinner with her and now didn't want her walking home alone?

The insult of it built like storm clouds on the horizon.

The *nerve* of that man. He looked at her like she was his favorite jelly on a croissant, then avoided her?

Julia hooked her arm through Morgan's. "Let's go."

As they started for the door, a new sense of insult rose in her. Not only did he not want to see her, but he also had somebody walk her home as if he was afraid she'd escape. He couldn't seem to let go of his commitment to her dad to watch her.

Okay. In fairness, she had almost bought a ticket to leave. But to *protect* him. Not to get away from him.

Alonzo and Julia deposited her at the door to the condo building and she rode up in the elevator in silence. She didn't even look at Riccardo's door, just powered through the hallway and into her own quarters.

Fuming, she fell into a fitful sleep but her phone rang what felt like only minutes later. She groggily said, "Hello?"

"It's time!" Julia's excited voice burst into Morgan's ear.

They'd talked about needing to pick the grapes very, very soon. "Probably tonight," Alonzo had said at dinner, and having lived on a vineyard most of her life, Morgan understood.

She whipped off the covers. "I'll be ready in five minutes."

"Someone will drive you back by ATV. Wear jeans."

Not taking even two seconds to think, Morgan jumped into jeans and a long-sleeve shirt. The heat of the day gave way to cooler nights and she wasn't taking any chances. In less than five minutes, she was in the hall, pressing the button for the elevator. Grapes had to be picked when they were at the perfect stage of ripeness. Once they hit the peak, a vintner had very little time to get them harvested. With a vineyard as large as the Ochoa family's that was a monumental task, especially harvesting by hand.

Waiting for the elevator, she didn't think about Riccardo, didn't glance at his door. He could sit and spin for all she cared.

The elevator finally came. She jumped in, rode to the first floor and raced out to the grounds of the main house. Nanna waved her over.

Walking to Riccardo's grandmother, she said, "*You're* picking grapes?"

"I haven't missed a year since I married Santiago and Carlos's father. I'm not stopping now."

Three ATVs pulled up to the cobblestone walk. Alonzo drove one. Julia drove the second. Riccardo drove the third.

Nanna gave her a quick shove. "Go on. I'll ride with Alonzo."

Annoyed that Riccardo had avoided her, she walked toward Julia's ATV.

But Riccardo caught her arm. "You come with me."

Before she could argue, someone else jumped on Julia's ATV.

She raised her chin and slid on behind Riccardo. "I'm surprised you're willing to take me."

He shoved the vehicle into gear. "Are you kidding? Let you alone among hundreds of people with access to the road?"

She couldn't believe he was still guarding her, couldn't believe he didn't understand that letting her run away would end his responsibility.

"You do realize that if I left you'd be off the hook?"

He turned around to gape at her. "Off the hook? Your father would shoot me."

"I am a twenty-five-year-old woman. All you have to do is tell him I wanted to leave and you didn't want to go to jail for holding me against my will."

For some reason she couldn't fathom, that made

him laugh. He turned around and hit the gas, and the ATV roared to life.

Out of stubbornness, she'd avoided sliding her arms around him. But as the thing bumped and jerked along the rough path, she had no choice. Forced, she slid her arms around his middle.

She closed her eyes, trying to dispel the tingles that whispered through her. In her mind's eye, she saw the abs her hands currently rested on. Wet from his shower the morning she'd seen him in only a towel.

She popped her eyes open to stop the vision, and saw they'd made it to the vineyard's staging area. Huge construction lights lit the rows of grapes, mimicking daylight. A cart held food and coffee. People stood in a huddle getting instructions from Santiago or lessons with the small shears required to cut the grape stems from Carlos. Trucks arrived with more pickers. Laughing townspeople and tourists piled out and headed to Alonzo for gloves, baskets and shears.

Riccardo got off the ATV and offered his hand to help Morgan off. She all but batted it away.

"I can get myself off an ATV."

"Fine. Let's go to my dad for instructions."

"On how to pick grapes?"

He sighed. "Yes."

"I grew up in a vineyard. I've picked grapes."

"Great. Then we'll go to Santiago for our assignment and Alonzo for our shears and baskets."

"Fine." Her head high, she marched to Santiago. He started giving her an assignment, but Riccardo took the sheet from his hands. "She's with me."

Santiago smiled and Morgan cursed old-world cultures that still thought women were helpless. Out of respect, she said nothing to Santiago, but when she and Riccardo were alone, heading back to his ATV after getting gloves and baskets from Alonzo, she snatched the paper from his hands.

"I can find my way alone."

"Or you could just get on the ATV and ride out with me."

Morgan stopped by the little red all-terrain vehicle. "Great. Nothing like feeling you're in prison."

Riccardo got on the ATV. "You're not in prison. You're free to do anything you want."

She slid on the ATV. "Really? I can leave tomorrow?"

"Absolutely. I'll come with you."

"The point is to get away from you."

"With the three hundred bucks you have left?"

Assuming she'd have his blessing, she'd intended to use his credit card, but she supposed that was off the table now.

She made a sound of exasperation as the ATV took off toward their assigned rows. He'd chase her down in Paris but wouldn't have dinner with her that night. Sure. That made sense.

When the vehicle stopped, she jumped off, grabbed her basket and shears and stormed to find her place.

But in the vines, her anger suddenly disappeared. The night was cool, not cold, and the air so refreshing she took a long breath to enjoy it. With her gloves on, she angled her shears on the stem of her first cluster of grapes and snipped. They fell into her hand and she set them in her basket, the way her mom had taught her when she was six.

"I see you do know how to do this."

"Did you think I was lying?" She wouldn't look at him. She knew he had some sort of conciliatory expression on his face and she'd add that to his good looks and instantly forgive him for refusing to be around her, for sticking her with Julia and

Alonzo and for basically telling her he'd follow her if she left. She didn't want to forgive him. She wanted him to like her.

There. She'd admitted it. She felt like a silly teenager with a crush on an older boy, but it was what it was. If she could figure out a way to get to Paris without him monitoring his own credit card, it wouldn't matter.

"I just thought that since it had been a while, you might have forgotten."

A new pain hit her. She remembered the night her mom had taught her where and how to cut the grape stem, her mom's laugh as it echoed through the vineyard and the many nights after that they'd picked together.

"You never forget the last thing you did with your mom."

Riccardo's heart stumbled to a stop. She'd tried to keep the sadness out of her voice, but he'd heard it. In all the time they'd spent together, she'd barely mentioned her mom.

"Why don't you tell me about her?"

She did the thing where her chin lifted and it almost made him laugh. She was like an adorable kitten trying to pretend she was a lion. His growing feelings for her spun through him again, but he easily stopped them. He'd spent most of the night reminding himself of the humiliation and embarrassment after Cicely canceled their wedding. Falling in the same trap twice would be infinitely worse. Able to keep himself in line now, he could spend time with her, even have fun with her.

"No, thank you."

"It's going to be a long night if we don't talk."

When she didn't reply, he said, "In all our conversations, you've never even told me her name."

"Montgomery."

"No. What was her first name?"

"Montgomery was her first name. It was her great-great-grandfather's last name. They gave her the name to honor him."

He chuckled. "And to make her life miserable in kindergarten."

Morgan shrugged. "She never mentioned that. She always talked about how she loved it. How it made her feel connected to her roots."

"I understand that." He felt the same way about his family. "Santiago and my father might be old-school sometimes, but my family is bound by tradition. Honor. A reason to make good grades at university. A reason to make my family proud."

She softened a bit. "Yes. That's obvious."

The noise of harvesters arriving to take their rows ebbed and flowed around them. Riccardo was sure that would cause Morgan to clam up. To his surprise, she kept talking.

"My mom was busy. A lawyer with some impressive clients. But she always made time for me. Every couple of months, we'd go shopping in Chicago."

He remembered her guessing they were going to Chicago when he'd told her they were going to Spain, and felt like a heel for not realizing there might have been a reason. He'd spent so much of their time together working not to fall for her that he'd missed some pretty important things.

They snipped more grapes, carefully laid them in their baskets.

"She taught me how to know what looked good on me and what didn't."

Eager to keep the conversation going, he said, "Which is why you have a great fashion sense."

She shook her head. "I seem to remember you

making fun of the clothes I bought at the airport and in the casino shops."

"I'm sure there wasn't much to choose from."

"You are such a charmer."

"Yet, you're mad at me."

"Because you don't trust me."

"The price of not going back to Lake Justice is being under my supervision. And it's not like I'm a hard taskmaster. You have your own rooms. You come and go with Nanna. If you want freedom, I'll arrange for the family jet to take you home."

Snipping a stem, Morgan considered taking him up on that. She was infinitely stronger than she had been the day she'd run from her wedding. She'd already talked to Charles. If her dad insisted on being in on the first conversation when she got home, it wouldn't make any difference. She could leave Riccardo Ochoa to the rest of his Vegas-going, probably womanizing life.

A little boy of about three came racing up to Riccardo. He tugged on his pant leg, talking in rushed Spanish that blew right by Morgan.

Riccardo reached down and swooped him up,

into his arms. Speaking clear, slow Spanish that Morgan easily understood, he said, "And how are you, Jesse?"

The little boy gave him an earnest look. "Do you have candy?"

Riccardo laughed and reached into his pocket, pulling out some individually wrapped treats. "Did you think I would forget?"

A woman wearing jeans and a T-shirt, with her dark hair caught up in a bandana, ran up to them. "I'm so sorry!" She took the little boy from Riccardo's arms. "Jesse! I told you to stay with me!"

"He's fine."

The woman's face softened. "Yes. Thank you." She lightly pinched her little boy's cheek. "Tell Riccardo thank you for the candy."

The little boy grinned shamelessly. "Thank you."

Morgan watched the exchange over the grape stems she snipped. He looked really good with a child. Very natural. He didn't have any nieces or nephews so she wondered how he'd gotten that way.

"You've very good with kids."

Watching the woman leave with her little boy, Riccardo said, "Yes. I like them."

The question that had burned inside her since watching him change a tire tumbled out. "How come you're not married?"

"I told you. I nearly was married. When it didn't work out, I changed my life." He shrugged. "It's kind of nice being rich and single. I can go where I want. Do what I want. I like being alone. Being my own person."

Her head tilted as she studied him. "Don't you feel you should be carrying on the family name?"

"My cousins are doing that."

"Don't your parents nag you about grandkids?"

He laughed. "Once in a while I get a sigh from my mother."

That made her laugh, too. "I'll bet."

"But I like being single. My life was compli-cated when I was engaged. Now it's easy. I don't want to go back."

Though their situations were totally different, she understood what he was saying. She didn't want to go back to her old life, either. No mat-ter how firm she was with her father, he was still Colonel Monroe, former secretary of state with high-powered friends and unfettered ambition. Like it or not, some of that would always spill over into her life.

If Riccardo didn't like complications, he didn't want her.

She wished that knowledge didn't sting so much, but it did. For the first time in her life she felt she was genuinely falling in love with somebody, and even if he had feelings for her, he didn't want them.

They said nothing for a few minutes as they snipped stems and filled baskets. Alonzo drove up in an ATV pulling a cart. He took their filled baskets and left empties. The conversations of the other pickers floated around them as a dull hum. Not clear enough to hear, but ever-present.

"You offered me your family jet a few minutes ago?"

He snipped a grape stem. "Yes?"

She took in a long breath, blew it out slowly. "I may want to take you up on it. I'm ready to talk to my dad, but I wouldn't mind a few days in Paris. That way, by the time I get home, he'll have left for his summit and I can meet with Charles privately." She shrugged. "You know. Give back the ring. That sort of thing."

He frowned. "I never saw you wearing a ring."

"I'd left it in my bedroom for the ceremony so we could get the wedding ring on without fumbling." She took another quick breath. "Anyway, when my dad gets home, everything will be settled with Charles and my discussions with my dad won't have to be about the wedding, but can be about our future as father and daughter."

"That makes sense."

"It really does."

"What are you going to say?"

"What we talked about on the highway, while you were fixing the tire. I'm going to say, 'Dad, I love you but we need some boundaries.'"

He laughed. "I didn't say that."

"I took your original idea and enhanced it."

"Do you know how you'll stand your ground?"

She stopped her scissors and looked across the grapes at him. "I'm moving out, remember?" She'd kissed him to thank him for helping her think it through, then he'd kissed her. Deeply, passionately, as if she was the second half of his soul.

He caught her gaze with dark eyes filled with longing. "Yes, I remember."

Her heart wanted to leap out of her chest, but no matter how much yearning she saw in his eyes, he wouldn't take the steps to fall in love with her.

She looked at her grapes again. "Yeah, well, that's why my first order of business will be to polish my résumé. I used Nanna's tablet that night to write it quickly. But it still needs some finessing."

"Do you have any idea where you want to work?"

"I think I've decided on New York City."

A few seconds passed with her heart beating heavily in her tight chest, as a new thought struck her. If she moved to New York City, they could find each other. It would be their chance to date, to have a normal opportunity to get to know each other. More time for him to realize he could have all those things he'd always wanted, to trust that she wouldn't leave him. That he could give her his heart.

All it would take would be one word of agreement from him now, one hint that he would see her when she was in New York City.

He said nothing.

Disappointment began to rise in her, but she quashed it. He could be too busy with the grapes to notice she was waiting for his reply.

She tried again. "Maybe you could help me find a job?"

"Maybe."

All her patience with him evaporated like night mist in the sun. "Maybe? Seriously! You drag me across an ocean to protect me from my dad but won't help me find a new job?"

He sighed. "Okay. Yes. Mitch and I know a lot of people. We could probably help you find a job."

"Sheesh. If it's that much trouble, don't bother!"

"Don't be mad."

"I'm not mad. I just thought we'd become friends."

They *had* become friends. And if he thought they could stay friends while he helped her find a job, helped her find a place to live, helped her adjust to city life, he would be all over it.

But what he saw in his head when he envisioned her being in his life in the city wasn't two friends. He saw himself stealing kisses, laughing at private jokes as they walked through condos with a real-estate agent, finding her in the tangles of his sheets and covers when they woke up the next morning. And one day she'd realize she'd gotten involved with a man before she was ready and she'd dump him. He'd been with Cicely for two long years, but even that hadn't been enough. There was no point in finding each other when she moved to the city. She needed years to heal and, like an idiot, Riccardo was falling in love now.

Though she was clearly exasperated with him, they finished their picking time talking about the nonthreatening topic of the places she'd like to work. It didn't surprise him that the United Nations appealed to her and he knew with her dad's background she could get a job without him. He expected to be relieved. Instead, it gave him an itchy feeling to realize just how little this woman needed him. His job, his money, meant nothing to her. She could have it all, get it all, without him. If she liked him, it was for himself. Not for anything he could give her. He guessed that was why he found her so appealing, and that made him doubly sorry that he had to let her go.

When their work was done, they returned to

the condo building. Getting out the elevator, they stepped into the hall where he'd almost kissed her, where she'd seen him in nothing but a towel, where he'd seen the interest in her eyes turn to awareness.

Ignoring the feelings that washed through him, he began punching in his key code. "Let me know when you want the plane."

"You really are going to let me go."

He shrugged, pretending he didn't understand what she was saying. "Now that I know your plan, I trust you. Just let me know when you want to go and I'll arrange it."

He peeked over and saw the sadness in her pretty blue eyes. Though it crushed him, he pushed open his door and walked away from her.

CHAPTER TEN

THE ALARM ON the old-fashioned clock woke Morgan a little after one on Monday afternoon. Before she'd fallen into bed, she'd taken a shower and slipped into a T-shirt and panties. After adding a pair of jeans, she ambled into the condo's main room and found a cart with coffee and some croissants and a note from Nanna telling her Lila and Mitch had arrived that morning and the women had congregated in Nanna's living room to talk.

She buttered a croissant and ate it as she found sandals, put them on and raced into the hall for the elevator. There was no sign of Riccardo as she waited for the little car, or on the first floor of the condo building or even the cobblestone walkway to the mansion. But it didn't matter. His mind was made up. He didn't even want to see her in New York City. He'd said he'd changed after being hurt and liked his life. He didn't want the complications of a relationship. It hurt, but she accepted it.

Done with her croissant, she ran up the big half-circle stairway and down the hall to Nanna's apartment.

She rang the bell, but didn't wait for anyone to answer. She walked inside and found her way to the sitting room where Nanna, Marguerite, Paloma, Julia and Lila's mom, Francine, sat with a small brunette with laughing eyes, who had to be Lila.

Nanna rose, kissed both her cheeks and turned her to face the new addition to their group. "This is Lila."

Lila stood up and gave her a hug. "You do realize there was a picture of you racing away from your wedding in all the London papers."

Morgan winced. "I'm sure the furor will die down soon."

Lila sat on the big ottoman between the sofa and a club chair and patted a spot beside her. "Sit."

She sat with Lila as Marguerite got her a cup of coffee. "Thanks."

"You're welcome. And thank you for helping with the harvest last night."

Lila looked from one woman to the next. "Oh, my gosh! You guys harvested last night?"

Paloma said, "Yes."

Morgan winced. "Am I the only one who took a nap?"

Marguerite laughed. "Probably."

Lila stood up. "Go, you guys! Seriously. We've been talking since I got here! You must be exhausted."

Nanna staunchly said, "We're fine."

"No, you're not," Lila insisted. "Go and get some sleep. You know I'm okay on my own."

"Actually," Morgan said, "I had a wonderful sleep."

Lila turned to her. "Great. We'll entertain each other while my husband talks business with his father and uncle."

Morgan said, "Sounds good."

After a round of hugs from everyone for Lila, the room cleared. Lila faced Morgan. "We should go to the pool."

Glad Nanna had insisted she buy a swimsuit, Morgan said, "I'd love that."

They left Nanna's residence and walked down the stairs and to the building with the two town houses. Lila pointed at it. "This is my stop. How about if we meet in ten minutes?"

"Okay."

Morgan raced back to her condo, put on her new one-piece swimsuit, sunglasses and the big sun hat and met Lila on the cobblestone path.

As they wandered to the huge blue pool surrounded by a sleek blue walkway and chaise lounges with aqua- and sand-colored pillows, Lila said, "I've never met a runaway bride before." She laughed. "Let alone one so famous."

"I'm not famous. My dad is."

"Well, you may not be famous in the way you think you are, but you're sort of the talk of the vineyard."

She winced. "Sorry. I don't mean to be trouble."

Lila took off her cover-up and sat on a chaise. "You're not trouble. Riccardo's mother and Marguerite are just sort of awestruck." She laughed. "No one's seen Riccardo spend this much time with one woman since Cicely."

Lila had the kind of earnest expression that inspired confidences and for two seconds Morgan was tempted to tell her she'd fallen head over heels for Riccardo. Instead, she stuck with the truth. "He thinks of me as a responsibility."

"I know! That's what makes it so funny. Paloma said apparently the only way to get Riccardo to stick with one woman is to put him in charge of her."

Glad she hadn't spilled her guts, Morgan said, "Is he really that bad?"

"He doesn't flaunt his affairs, if that's what you mean. He's discreet and happy."

"So he says."

"It's a shame, though, because before Cicely, he wanted the whole deal. Wife, kids, a summer house at the beach." She thought for a second. "In a way, it's like he's half the person he used to be."

She remembered him with the little boy in the vineyard. "He told me that before Cicely he wanted to be married."

"He did." Lila leaned closer. "In fact, I think that was why he took up with her. He was more in love with the idea of starting his family than with her."

"Was she pretty?"

Lila's face softened. "Only someone interested in Riccardo would ask that question."

"It doesn't matter. He told me he wouldn't get involved with a woman on the rebound—and since I just broke up with my fiancé, I guess I am. But, worse, he's also said he likes his life just as it is. When I mentioned moving to New York City for a fresh start, he didn't even want to help me find a job."

Lila's mouth opened in disbelief. "He likes you."

"As a friend."

Lila shook her head. "No. For him to be so cautious, he must really be getting feelings for you."

"Yeah, well, it soon won't matter. He's offered me the family jet to go home."

Lila caught her hand. "You can't! Riccardo is such a wonderful guy and it's broken my heart to watch him go through everything that happened with Cicely. But the real tragedy is that he intends to live his entire life without what he really wants. If he likes you, he could be getting back to normal."

"No. This is fate, Lila. We met at the absolute wrong time. I have trouble with my dad to straighten out. I just broke an engagement. I'm everything he hates."

Lila laughed. "I doubt that."

"Yeah, well, if he should decide to change his mind, he can find me in New York."

Lila shook her head sharply. "That's where he hides. He'll drown himself in work until he feels okay again, then pick up his old life where he left off. You have to do something now."

Morgan said, "I can't." Because it was true. She might be falling in love with Riccardo, but she wouldn't force him into anything, lead him into anything. That's what her father and Charles had done with her. She refused to lure him into a relationship. He had to come to her of his own volition.

Dinner that night was at Santiago and Marguerite's. Riccardo had worked late so he wasn't surprised there was no answer when he knocked on Morgan's door. She'd probably gone to the main house herself. He walked over to the mansion, his hands in his trouser pockets, the moon a sliver of light in the sky.

When he pressed the buzzer announcing his arrival, a butler opened the door for him. Mitch's parents were old-school and still made good use of the household staff, which added to the formal atmosphere when Riccardo entered their sitting room.

His eyes unerringly found Morgan. He told himself he only looked for her because it was part of his job. But his breath stumbled when he saw her. Her pale green dress somehow made her big blue eyes more dramatic and accented her long yellow hair. She sat on the ottoman with Lila, with Mitch on the sofa behind them. From the easy camaraderie between Morgan and Lila it was clear they'd been introduced and had begun getting to know each other.

He had the sudden, unexpected sense that his duty to her was over. In the same way that her calling Charles had made her feel free, having Mitch home freed him from being solely in charge of their best customer's daughter.

"Good evening, everyone." He took a seat on a club chair across from a long sofa where Nanna, his parents and Marguerite sat. Santiago relaxed on the second club chair. Francine sat on the third.

"You're late," Nanna scolded.

"I was working."

Mitch said, "On what?"

"I've gone through all our customer accounts so

you have real numbers on which wines are selling the best. Just in case you have to make some phone calls."

Marguerite groaned. "No work at dinner!"

Riccardo's mom seconded that. "Family time is family time!"

That was when it hit him that his entire family was in the room. With the addition of Julia, then Lila and her mom, the group had swelled in what seemed like the blink of an eye.

Something soft and warm rippled through him. The family that had almost been blown apart when Alonzo stole Julia from Mitch had healed itself in the most magnificent way.

The butler announced dinner and they filed into the dining room. Everyone took seats, leaving him and Morgan beside each other again.

Calmer and more comfortable than he'd been in a long time, he pulled out Morgan's chair for her. He'd ended any possibility of a romance between them and he'd cemented that by being neutral with her while they harvested grapes. He might be pining for what they could have had, but she looked adapted. As if what he'd been saying to her had finally sunk in.

She sat, giving him a smile over her shoulder. "Thank you."

He took the chair beside her. "You're welcome."

With so much family, one big conversation wasn't convenient. The discussion split in half. Nanna, Mitch's parents and Riccardo's parents talked about past harvests. Alonzo, Julia, Mitch and Lila talked about Greece, one of the places Mitch and Lila had visited on their honeymoon. Morgan easily slid into that discussion and Riccardo soon followed suit.

After dinner was eaten, Alonzo rose and tapped his spoon against his wineglass. "Everyone," he said, calling everyone's attention to him. "I…" He glanced at Julia. "*We* have an announcement."

Julia's face reddened sweetly, endearingly, and Riccardo knew what was coming.

"I'm pregnant!"

Marguerite put her hand on her chest. "I'm going to be a grandmother?"

Santiago pulled in a sharp breath. "Our next generation begins," he said reverently, then he rose, picking up his wineglass for a toast. *"Salude!"*

Riccardo glanced at Morgan. Tears filled her

eyes, but they were happy tears. He suddenly, unexpectedly pictured her with her own kids and his breath caught.

He could see her with a little blonde girl and a dark-haired boy.

He shook his head to clear it. He didn't want to think about her that way.

Because it would mean she was happy with another man.

He might be able to let her go, but he wasn't a saint. He did not want to see her future.

CHAPTER ELEVEN

FROM THAT POINT on Riccardo kept himself away from her as much as possible. Imagining her with children was too painful to contemplate. He couldn't handle any more goodbyes at doors, or conversations that only reminded him how perfect she was. Nothing could change the fact that she wasn't even two weeks out of a relationship, that she would go home to a new life, with a new attitude, and want her freedom to enjoy it all.

The night of the ball, he walked out of his condo, dressed in his tux. No one had told him to escort Morgan, but it was simply common sense that he should.

Preparing himself to see her looking wonderful in her gown, he knocked on her door and waited. When there was no answer, he knocked again and waited again. It was too late for her to be in the shower, too late for the noise of a hair dryer to be drowning him out.

She had to have already left for the ball.

Misery invaded his chest. He tried to deny it but he'd been looking forward to escorting her tonight. She'd be leaving the next day. He'd probably never see her again, and he'd missed the chance to walk her over.

After a short ride in the elevator, he stepped out into the warm evening. He looked up the cobblestone path thinking she might only be a little ahead of him.

And she was…on the arm of his cousin Lorenzo.

Fury shuddered through him before he could stop it. He couldn't believe his mother had called her sister to get an escort for Morgan. The insult of it rattled along his bones, ignited his blood.

Entering the mansion through the front door, so he could go through the receiving line, he first greeted Mitch's parents, then Mitch and Lila.

After hugging Mitch and kissing Lila's cheek, he said, "You look radiant."

Always the kidder, Mitch said, "Thank you."

"Even on your best day, you're not radiant," Riccardo said, then he turned to Lila. "This is when we officially say welcome to the family."

"Thanks," Lila said through the soft laugh she'd only found once she and Mitch had become serious. Her face glowed with happiness. So did Mitch's, if Riccardo allowed himself to be honest.

Longing rippled through him. Not for marriage or kids, but for that connection. Since Cicely he'd believed it trite, or maybe something for other men, but getting to know Morgan had awakened all those yearnings again.

He turned to leave the receiving line and saw Morgan laughing with Lorenzo. Stealing his night. But he knew the anger that shuffled through him was wrong.

He walked directly to the bar. "Whiskey."

He named a brand that cost enough to make most people's heads spin. But he didn't care. He'd helped Morgan get through her problems, brought her to Spain, and he wouldn't even get twenty minutes with her tonight before she boarded a plane tomorrow.

"She's over there."

The sound of his grandmother's voice almost made him drop his drink. When he realized

Nanna was talking about Morgan, he wanted to pour his very expensive whiskey over her head.

"Why would you be pointing out Morgan to me when the family invited someone else to be her escort?"

Nanna looked confused. "You were just mumbling about someone getting on a plane tomorrow, I assumed you were talking about Morgan."

Damn it! Now his craziness was spilling over into reality.

"She looks pretty in that dress, doesn't she?"

He glanced over and saw the front view of gorgeous Morgan Monroe in a tight yellow gown. Though he'd followed her up the cobblestone walk to the ballroom, he'd only seen the full train in the back. He hadn't realized the dress beneath was formfitting.

"Yellow's her color."

"I like her in blue." He mumbled that, so his grandmother wouldn't hear it. Louder, he said, "I should go say hello to Lorenzo."

Nanna grabbed his arm before he could move. "No. We're getting ready to eat. And you're at the main family table, so you can escort me over."

He said, "Okay," then wondered where Morgan

would be sitting. But even as the question popped into his head, he realized that's why his mother had called Lorenzo. Morgan wasn't family—or even extended family, as Lila's mom was—so she wouldn't be sitting at the family table.

Lorenzo had been called upon to entertain her.

The relief that poured through him made him laugh. No one was keeping them apart. No one had seen him falling for Morgan. His thoughts had been nothing but his own imaginings. He'd been foolish to get so worked up.

The dinner sped by amid toasts to Lila and Mitch. When the dancing started, he had every intention of asking Morgan to dance, just to show himself he was fine—making mountains out of molehills because of stupid feelings he shouldn't have. He also wanted a minute to talk to her about her arrangements for the next day, when she went home.

But when he finally found a chance to slide in and ask her, she looked at him with her earnest blue eyes and his heart stumbled in his chest.

No matter how much he told himself he didn't want the feelings he had for her, he had them. He wouldn't do anything about them. She was only two weeks out of a bad relationship. And he didn't want to end up with a broken heart.

Still…

Was it wrong to want to have a few hours with her? Was it wrong to want another kiss? Just one more kiss? He'd paid the price of rescuing her from her dad, flying her to Spain, connecting her to women who could help her move on…

Didn't he deserve this night?

One measly kiss?

He swore to himself that he wouldn't hurt her or let himself get hurt. He wouldn't touch her beyond a kiss, but they deserved a night—one night, one kiss—before she left.

An ache built inside him, not just to touch her, but also for the innocence Cicely had stolen from him. What he wouldn't give to see only Morgan's goodness, the fun they could have together, the life they could create, and not the myriad consequences that could rain down on him when the whole damn thing imploded.

Because it would. She couldn't have real feelings for him. She would go home and soon forget everything that happened between them.

But he wouldn't. He'd remember her forever.

* * *

Morgan had spent the entire night watching Riccardo over Lorenzo's shoulder. She didn't know why he seemed to be spending the majority of his time at the bar, but her heart skipped a beat when she saw him walking toward her and Lorenzo. And suddenly he was there.

He nodded to her. "Morgan."

She said, "Good evening," but told her heart to settle down. If there was one thing she'd learned about the Ochoa family, it was that they were steeped in tradition, polite to a fault. Coming over to say hello, Riccardo was only being courteous. He'd made his feelings about her very clear. And stayed away from her for days to prove he meant it. She would not make a fool of herself.

He shook Lorenzo's hand. "And it's good to see you, too, cousin."

Lorenzo smiled. "My pleasure."

"I wonder if you would mind if I had a few dances with your date."

Her heart did the funny, shivery thing again. She told it to stop. This was nothing but a duty to Riccardo.

Lorenzo all but bowed. "Of course."

"Actually, because we're in side-by-side condos, it makes sense for me to walk her home, too."

Lorenzo said, "That's not necessary."

"No, but it's my pleasure." Riccardo laughed. "I'm releasing you of your duty. Go," he said, motioning around the room at the elegant crowd, which included eligible women. "Enjoy yourself."

Though he didn't look pleased, Lorenzo walked away.

Riccardo faced her. "I'd love a dance."

She'd love an explanation. But she wasn't about to ask him for one and embarrass herself. If he wanted to dance with her and walk her home, it wasn't to enjoy her company. It was only out of respect for his family's sense of honor.

She curtsied, the way she'd been taught by her mother when she was very, very young, and the gesture was mannerly. "The pleasure is mine."

The band began playing a waltz and she smiled politely as he took her into his arms. As the smooth material of his tux slid across her hands, her breath stuttered in and fluttered out. Every man in attendance wore a tuxedo, yet not one of them looked as casually elegant, as sex-on-a-spoon gorgeous as Riccardo.

"Are you enjoying the evening?" Damn! She sounded like a hostess at one of her dad's stuffy parties.

His head tilted. "I think the better question is are you enjoying it?"

"Yes." Her voice came out as a nervous squeak and she had to fight not to squeeze her eyes shut in misery. In that second, part of her was glad her dad had sheltered her from this. The other part was still miffed. If she'd had the normal teenage girl experiences with boys, she wouldn't be making a fool of herself right now. "You're an excellent dancer."

"Part of my training."

She smiled. "Mine, too."

As he expertly swirled her around the room, her nervousness seemed to float away.

Just when she thought she would be okay, he caught her gaze. "You look amazing tonight. Do you know you're probably the most beautiful woman I've ever met?"

That made her laugh. "Really? You're going to use lines on me?" But part of her wanted to believe it. He was the most handsome man she'd ever met. He'd totally redefined sexy for her.

No, actually, what he'd done was introduce her to sexy. In a world where everybody wore Oxford cloth shirts and chinos he was silk and swagger.

He swung her around. "I would never use a line on you."

"Oh, now, I think you're just lying."

"Okay, say I didn't mind falling back on a line or two every once in a while. In this instance, it's not a line. You are the most beautiful woman I've ever met."

The song ended and they stopped dancing, but their gazes clung. The whole world shifted. Just as he had introduced her to sexy, he was changing something else in her world. Not the way she saw herself, but how she saw relationships. What it was supposed to be like between a man and a woman.

There was a closeness, almost an arc of electricity connecting them. Capturing them. Making her feel linked to him, open to anything he wanted, as the world—a world she never knew existed—came to quivering life.

The music began again. This time it was a slow song. He pulled her close, nestled her against him and her eyes drifted shut as the sensation of being held to him trembled through her.

They danced the rest of the set knitted together or an arm's distance apart. Their arc in place. Their connection never broken.

Too soon, the guests of honor left, along with their parents, then Nanna and Riccardo's parents.

Alonzo gave a good-night toast, then took Julia's hand and escorted her from the ballroom, ending the party.

The crowd dispersed, everyone heading out the front entry to gather wraps or hats. Riccardo faced her. "We can leave through the private entry."

"Yes. Thank you. That would be great."

She stumbled over the words because she had no idea what would happen next. Their doors were side by side, bedrooms a whisper away. It seemed totally wrong to end a night of being held any other way than making love.

So nervous she thought she'd die from it, Morgan held out her arm. "I'm ready."

He gave her a long look. Everything inside her shivered, as she realized the double meaning she might have given him. Still, it was what she wanted.

After a beat, he took her arm and led her to the doors in the back.

But he said nothing.

She sucked in a breath to still her nerves and hopefully strengthen her voice. "I'm guessing this is a shortcut."

"Yes. To the back entrance."

"Okay."

They reached the discreet double doors and he opened them. They walked to the condos under the dark sky. Clouds hid the stars, promising rain in a few hours. He released her arm and opened the condo building door, granting her entry first.

She smiled. "Thank you."

At the elevator, he pressed the button, and the doors opened automatically. She stepped inside. So did he.

They rode in silence and goose bumps appeared on her arms. For as sure as she was that the evening should end in lovemaking, nerves changed her mind. They'd only known each other two weeks. They'd kissed once. She was crazy to think he wanted to sleep with her.

She was never so grateful as when the elevator stopped on the second floor and she could race out. When she reached her door, she turned to say a polite goodbye, but he was right behind her and she almost bumped in to him.

His eyes were as black and intense as the sky had been. "You're running away?"

Her chest tightened.

He took a step closer. "Why?"

The reasoning in her head in the elevator had sounded so good. But here? At her door? Caught in the gaze of his dark, brooding eyes…she couldn't remember a word of it. "I'm not sure."

"I think you're avoiding my question."

"No. It just was a long night and I think I'm confused."

"About?"

She sucked in a breath. "You want me to say it? To admit that I think there's only one way this night should end?"

"No. I want you to tell me that you're attracted to me." His voice cascaded over her like warm honey. He took the final step that separated them. "I want you to tell me that you want me to kiss you."

She did. Oh, good God, she did. But he didn't move. Didn't say anything else. And she realized he really was waiting for her.

"I do."

He leaned closer. "You do what?"

"I want you to kiss me."

CHAPTER TWELVE

THE KISS BYPASSED being warm and sweet and went directly to hot and steamy. Morgan didn't care. Every cell in her body tingled to life as if awakening from a long, unnecessary sleep, and she wanted more. She rolled to her tiptoes, put her hands on each side of his face and indulged.

Their tongues twined. Stuttering breaths mingled. His hands slid down her bare back, hesitating at the bustle-topped train of her gown as if frustrated, then slowly cruising up her naked skin again, raising goose bumps. When he reached the slim straps at the edges of her shoulders, his fingers skimmed beneath the satiny material but stopped. The kiss slowed. The heated encounter reduced to soft brushes. Harsh breaths leveled. Their lips pulled apart as he raised his head.

Morgan opened her eyes to find his squeezed shut. He popped them open with a muttered curse.

"This is wrong."

"Really?" Her slight whisper filled the small lobby, as frustration filled her. All she could think about was touching him. Kissing him. Belonging to him. She couldn't believe he thought this was wrong.

"I shouldn't be forcing you in to this."

Confused, she just looked at him. "Forcing me?"

"Tempting you?" He smiled ruefully. "Right now, when you're scared and confused I seem like the answer to all your problems. But as soon as you get home, move to New York City, get a new job, you'll put all this behind you."

She listened to every word he said, twisted them around, searching for meaning, and eventually said, "You don't think there's something between us?"

He shrugged. "I know there's something between us, but I also know you're going home tomorrow and we're probably never going to see each other again. It would be so easy to fall into bed together, but then you'd regret it."

"Regret it?" Her heart kicked against her ribs. "I waited my whole life to feel what I felt with you tonight."

He shook his head. "You're going to feel a hundred different things when you get home. And one of them is going to be happiness that you didn't do anything to mess up your life."

"My life already was messed up."

"No, I mean that you didn't make any commitments, any promises." He caught her gaze. "You really will be able to start over when you get home."

She turned that over in her head until she remembered that the real bottom line was that he might have feelings for her but he didn't want them.

Hadn't he said it a million times?

And he was strong enough to fight them.

Because he liked his life simple. No complications.

She stared at him, feeling like an idiot as her heart splintered into a million pieces. Not only had she found her first love; she was getting her first heartbreak.

She stepped back. "You know what? You're right." She smiled at him as her pride swelled, refusing to let her try to convince him he was wrong for fear that she'd beg. Love was new for her. The all-encompassing sensations told her she was in over her head, not experienced enough to handle it and certainly not experienced enough to walk into a situation with someone who didn't feel the same as she did.

The pain of just the thought almost paralyzed her.

She pulled in a breath. "Thank you for a lovely evening."

She heard Riccardo say, "You're welcome," as she turned and walked into her apartment. Her gown shivered and swished as she went directly to the phone. She dialed the number for the household staff and not only ordered a limo, but she also asked if the family jet had been reserved for her. A manager came to the phone and assured her that it was blocked off for her use and if her plans had changed it could be available to her in two hours, the time it would take to get a pilot.

She thanked him and hung up the phone.

Then she let herself cry. For being naive. For being so lonely she'd fallen for the first man who was kind to her. And for being back to being lonely again.

When her tears slowed, she almost began packing. Then she realized she wanted nothing that would remind her of this time. She might have fallen in love but it had been a foolish thing to do, the silly, heartbreaking meanderings of someone who had imploded her life and then set about to pick up the pieces and restore some semblance of normality.

But in her naiveté, she'd fallen for the man who had helped her, and he'd had to tell her what a fool she was.

Riccardo woke the next morning a little after ten, ran his hands down his face and dressed for breakfast with the family. Everyone had been out late the night before so the meal would be more of a brunch. They'd laugh and talk about the ball, mostly gossip, but good-natured gossip. His nanna loved to talk about a party as much as she loved to attend one. Everyone would be there, including Morgan.

He paused at her door before shaking his head and walking to the elevator. She wouldn't want to see him. And he shouldn't want to see her. He couldn't believe he'd been so desperate as to want one real night with her. But he had. And then it had taken the willpower of a saint to pull away from her.

And that kiss?

Walking to the main house, he reminded himself he couldn't think about that kiss. This morning, he had to appear unaffected. Nonchalant. He'd just barely gotten them out of a potentially sticky situation at her door the night before. He didn't want to hurt her now.

But the kiss had been everything. He'd probably remember those few hours at the ball for the rest of his life. He'd probably always wonder what it would have been like if he could have taken the next step.

Sadly, though, he knew there was only one answer to that. She'd realize two or three months—or maybe two years, as Cicely had—into their future that she'd fallen for him out of need, necessity, when she was vulnerable, and she'd break it off.

It was better to part now.

He trudged up the stairway and down the hall, upset with himself, but ready to be cool and distant. He rang the bell and let himself in. Everyone was already in the dining room. He took his seat at the end of the table, and realized that for the first time since he'd brought Morgan to the Ochoa home, he didn't have someone to sit beside.

Mitch was the first to notice him. "Well, look who the cat dragged in."

"Cats didn't have to drag me anywhere," he replied with a laugh. "I danced off my whiskey." He almost added, *Where's Morgan?* His tongue itched to say the words, but his brain reminded him that he wasn't supposed to care. To his family, he was nothing more than her caretaker.

Julia sighed. "Everybody stop talking about drinking. I had to pass up France's best champagne last night."

"Poor baby," Mitch teased.

But Alonzo took her hand and kissed the knuckles. "It will be worth it."

Julia's entire demeanor changed as she gazed into his eyes. "It will."

Riccardo had never seen Mitch look at Julia the way Alonzo did. But more important, he'd never seen Julia look at Mitch the way she looked at Alonzo.

He shook his head to clear it of the thought that had seemed to come out of nowhere, and when he did, his gaze collided with the empty chair beside his.

He couldn't believe she was missing her last meal with the family. He wondered if Morgan was sick—then he remembered she'd turned away rather quickly the night before. Maybe the break he'd thought so simple hadn't been? Maybe she was so upset she didn't want to eat breakfast with his family?

An odd sense tumbled through him, regret so intense he could barely breathe. He never, ever, ever wanted to hurt her.

"So, Riccardo, I'm surprised you're here," Nanna said, then sipped her tea. "The limo's scheduled to take Morgan to the airport in ten minutes. I thought you'd accompany her."

That news cut through him like a knife. She wasn't supposed to leave until two. He'd hoped to catch a glimpse of her. To say goodbye.

Julia teared up. "I am so sorry to see her go."

Lila said, "Me, too. Did she invite you to the girls' weekend in Paris?"

Paloma said, "I think she invited all of us. Mani-pedis and margaritas."

The women laughed.

His father said, "I'll miss her."

Santiago said, "Me, too. I don't think anybody's ever hugged me goodbye quite that hard."

Marguerite said, "Best guest we've ever had."

Everybody laughed, but Riccardo's blood stopped pumping through his veins. Though he kept himself from embarrassing himself, he couldn't stop his brain from jumping to the obvious conclusion.

She left without saying goodbye to him.

She'd said goodbye to everybody but him.

He'd brought her here, talked her through everything in her life, wanted to kiss her so many times he'd ached from it...then she left without saying goodbye?

It hurt. Oddly. Passionately. So deeply his muscles trembled. But he forced himself not to care. He couldn't care. What they had was some sort of temporary thing a woman got for a man who helped her. She did not love him. She had needed him.

Twenty minutes later, he, Mitch, Alonzo and

their fathers walked out of Nanna's home, down the circular stairway and toward the conference room.

Riccardo said nothing as his cousins and uncle talked about the third vineyard. Mostly how they would pay for it since Alonzo and Julia would need a house, a big house for the children they planned to have. He wasn't brooding over Morgan not saying goodbye. Technically, they'd said their goodbyes the night before—

But he felt empty. At a loss. He'd guarded her, protected her from her dad, brought her to his family. Enjoyed her company. Shared kisses that had touched his soul—

Didn't he deserve a goodbye?

The answer crept into his conscious. He would have deserved a goodbye if he hadn't hurt her the night before. He hadn't seen it at the time, because he was so grateful he had the strength to pull himself away from her. But looking back, remembering how she'd walked into her condo, he saw it. The droop of her shoulders. The sadness in her eyes.

They reached the conference room door but before his father could open it, the sound of his grandmother calling his name echoed down the corridor.

"Riccardo! Riccardo!"

All five men stopped. When she reached them, she said, "I'd like a moment with Riccardo."

Santiago said, "Of course."

Puzzled, Riccardo stepped out of the way to let his father, uncle and cousins pass. His dad closed the door behind them.

Nanna said, "Go after her."

"What?"

"Go after Morgan. She's only got a short head start. They have to load her bags, run preflight checks. If you take one of Mitch's motorcycles, you can catch her before the plane takes off."

"No. I don't want to catch her." He did. He desperately did. He wanted to tell her he was sorry for hurting her. He wanted to kiss her senseless. Beg her to stay. "I don't know what you think you saw happening between us, but I kept her from being another Cicely. I rescued Morgan and she was grateful. But neither of us did anything we'd regret. And when she gets home and is settled in New York City, she'll thank me. She'll realize what she thought was happening between us was only appreciation."

Nanna's brow winkled. "Is that what you think?"

"It's what I know. I went through this with Cicely, remember?"

"I remember Cicely, but I also remember that she loved her ex. Always loved her ex."

Riccardo just looked at her.

"Morgan didn't love Charles. At best, she thought of him as a friend. Are you saying you're letting her go because of Charles?"

"No. I'm letting her go because she's only two weeks out of her relationship."

"No, she's two weeks out of a prison her dad created for her."

He ran his hand across the back of his neck, remembering that she'd barely spoken about Charles. That her concern had always been for her dad. Not losing her dad. She might have wanted to see Charles, but it had been to give back the ring. To set things straight.

Still…

"It doesn't matter. An engagement is an engagement and she just ended hers."

His grandmother heaved a long-suffering sigh.

"So you're willing to let her go back to her fiancé?"

"She's not going back to her fiancé."

"You think not?" Nanna's eyes narrowed. "You hurt her. Only a complete moron would have missed it when we said goodbye this morning. She talked about seeing Charles, about how nice it would be to talk to him." Nanna shook her finger at him. "You thought you were a rebound for her? Charles is going to be the real rebound man. She'll go home to Charles, who will comfort her, and that will be how they will get back together."

He thought about everything she'd gone through. How her freedom had been so hard-won. "She wouldn't— I mean she might revert to some of her old behaviors with her dad. But she's a new person. She wouldn't want her old fiancé back."

"Maybe."

There were too many options in that one little word. The possibilities spun through his brain.

"Think it through. The fiancé she left will be the one to help her pick up the pieces from the broken heart *you* gave her."

Riccardo shook his head. "That's all wrong. Backward. She needed help getting away from him. I gave it to her. I can't be the reason she ends up with him."

"Then go after her."

"I can't!"

"Oh, Riccardo." Nanna's eyes softened. "If you don't, you will not get another chance. You will lose another love."

When he said nothing, not wanting anyone to realize how quickly he'd fallen for her, she caught his forearm. "I saw how you looked at her."

He thought of Alonzo and Julia and wondered if that's how he'd looked at Morgan. With his heart in his eyes.

"I saw how she looked at you. Like a woman who's found the one man she wants to spend the rest of her life with."

Just the thought that she might really love him opened his heart. Air began filling his lungs again.

"If you've never trusted me about anything else. Trust me on this, *Nene*."

"I do trust you."

He finally saw what she saw. They might not have known each other long, but she'd been a blank slate when he met her. Not a woman pining for a man who had left her, but a woman who had no idea what love was.

He'd realized he was falling for her the night before he shuffled her off to Spain. If this empty ache in his chest was any indication, the falling was over and he was in love.

And he'd let her go.

Morgan's car sat in the lot of the municipal airport right where she'd left it. She jumped in and began the short drive to her father's vineyard.

She was strong now. Wise and strong. There was no point in going to Paris, waiting the two days before her dad's trip to Stockholm. Her dad would be at the house when she got there.

She didn't care. She was in the throes of her first heartbreak. She'd stupidly fallen in love in two weeks. With a man who didn't want to be in love. Another woman would turn to her father for comfort. She girded herself to prepare for his wrath.

Though part of her thought her dad was the one who might need to prepare himself for her. She wasn't the sheep who'd run from her wedding. She would speak her mind.

She pulled the car in front of the house, got out and headed for the main door. She stopped and took a breath. Then she twisted the knob, gave a push and called, "I'm home."

Her father started down the quietly elegant wooden stairway, Charles behind him. "We know. We saw someone open the gate and alerted security. You're lucky you weren't arrested."

He reached the bottom of the stairs. She longed to throw herself into his arms, to tell him her heart had been broken, to get the comfort only a father could give.

She straightened her shoulders. "It's nice to see you, too, Dad."

"You're not getting snippy with me, are you?"

"No, but I'm also not going to play sheep anymore."

His face contorted in confusion. "Sheep?"

"You and I will talk in a minute." She looked past him, smiled warmly. "Charles."

He reached out and hugged her, a soft, sweet hug that spoke of their friendship. She almost broke down. But they had things to talk about. She called upon the well of reserves she had way deep down inside her to keep her composure.

"Let's go into the den."

Charles said, "Sure."

They headed to her dad's den and the Colonel exploded. "What is going on here!"

"I'm going to talk to Charles, to apologize in person. Then I'm going to talk to you."

"No! No! No!" her dad sputtered. "I've spent two weeks apologizing for you! I'll have my time now!"

"I never asked you to apologize for me. But more than that, even you should respect Charles's right to get a better explanation than the brief apology I gave him over the phone."

She turned and walked with Charles into the den.

Riccardo counted the minutes it took to get from the small Lake Justice municipal airport to Monroe Vineyards. He'd gotten to his family's private airstrip a few minutes too late and cursed Morgan's ability to get away. He'd made a few calls and finally got a jet from a family friend and told the pilot to punch it, yet he'd still arrived in the United States an hour after Morgan.

When he got to the gate for Monroe Vineyards,

he scanned his brain for the code to get inside, hoping they hadn't changed it since the night after Morgan's wedding, when he'd met with the Colonel to talk about him going after her. He punched in two sets of numbers before he got it right and suspected the wrong attempts had probably set off an alarm, but he didn't care. He raced to the house, jumped out of his rental vehicle and ran to the front door.

When he stepped into the quiet, formal foyer, he met Colonel Monroe. "You're the second person today to get inside my compound without my authorization."

"You should change more than one number when you reset your gate lock."

"There are twenty-four digits in that code. How did you know that I only changed one number? Better yet, how did you know what number changed?"

He hadn't. He'd guessed. Still, he pointed at his temple. "Mind like a steel trap." He looked around frantically. "Where's Morgan?"

"Talking to Charles in the den. Seriously, they've been in there an hour. I tried to get in twice—she threated to disown me. What the hell did you do to her, son?"

"They've been in there an hour?"

"Yes! I think—"

"Don't think!" he said, suddenly understanding Morgan's frustration that day she'd told him not to think. "Which way is the den?"

"Down that hall and to the right, but—"

Riccardo didn't hear the rest of what the Colonel said. He ran down the hall and whipped open the door. "Don't get back together with him! You belong to me!"

It took a second for his surroundings to sink in, to see the brown leather sofa, huge mahogany desk, cold fireplace and two shell-shocked people.

"Riccardo?"

The man Riccardo assumed was Charles turned to Morgan. "This is Riccardo?"

"Yes."

He shook his head with a laugh as he rose. He leaned down and kissed Morgan's cheek. "We'll talk again."

Riccardo's blood all but boiled. "No. You won't."

Charles laughed and left the room.

* * *

Morgan rose from the brown leather chair. "I belong to no one." She said the words quietly, succinctly, but inside her heart thundered. She didn't consider belonging to him as being a possession, but more of a commitment. But he'd hurt her, confused her so many times, he had some explaining to do.

He caught her hands, brought them to his cheeks. "I'm sorry."

"Sorry?" Fear raced through her. That didn't sound like the declaration of a man who wanted her to belong to him.

He let go of her hands and ran his fingers through his hair. "I'm saying this all wrong." He squeezed his eyes shut. "When you were gone this morning, I wouldn't admit it, even to myself, but I hit rock-bottom. Worse than when Cicely left me. I loved you in a way I'd never loved anyone. We had little more than a handful of days, and half of them I tried to stay away from you, yet I loved you."

Her heart pounded in her chest. Her throat closed. The urge to tell him she loved him, too, bubbled up then bubbled over, but she fought to keep her mouth closed. She might be new at running her own life, but she knew what she wanted. Truth. Honesty. Reality. She wouldn't misinterpret him again.

"What happened to the worry that our relationship was just some sort of rebound thing?"

"My nanna reminded me of a few things. Mostly that you hadn't loved Charles. You'd left a trap not a relationship. Your feelings and Cicely's would have been totally different."

"Thanks... I think."

He shook his head. "Don't you get it? What happened between us was real."

Tears of happiness filled her eyes. "It certainly feels that way to me."

"When Julia said she was pregnant I could see you with a child, *our* child." He took a step closer. "That's why I was so afraid to be around you."

She smiled. "That's very romantic."

"Then there were the times I almost kissed you."

Her smile grew. "Those were nice." She raised her eyes to meet his. "But the actual kissing was better."

He laughed. "Infinitely better."

It was all so terrifyingly wonderful that Morgan needed the words. The real words. Spoken clearly. On their own. Not as part of an explanation.

"And you love me?"

"Yes. I love you."

A laugh spilled out. Relief and joy collided and danced. "I love you, too."

"And you're sure?"

She laid her hands on his chest, reveling in the fact that all this was real. He was hers. They were going to start a new life. A rich, wonderful life of family and honesty. There would be no more pretending to be somebody she wasn't.

"Riccardo, I've had twenty-five years of being who everybody else thought I should be. You're the first person who was worth fighting to be myself for."

He laughed, then put both hands on her cheeks and kissed her, his mouth both clever and desperate. As it sunk in for both of them that this was real, the kiss slowed. Desperation became tenderness.

When they finally broke apart, he said, "I think we should get married."

"I think we should date. I don't mistrust what I

feel, but I'd actually like to have the experience of dating."

He thought about that. "You are moving to New York City?"

"Yes. But I'm thinking of getting my own apartment."

He caught her around the waist and tugged her to him. "Not a chance."

Then he kissed her again until her blood warmed and any worry she had about him disappeared. And she knew they were going to have a wonderful life, just as surely as she knew her dad would have one of his fits when he heard the news.

But they could handle him.

They could handle anything.

EPILOGUE

RICCARDO AND MORGAN married almost exactly a year later. The day of her wedding, she didn't have a mom to help her dress, but she had a nanna, three moms—Paloma, Marguerite and Francine—and Lila and Julia.

"I wanted her hair up." Julia pouted as she hoisted her three-month-old son on her hip.

"You hush," Paloma said. "Riccardo likes her hair down."

Julia gasped, horrified. "Morgan, please tell me you are not going to be one of those wives who does everything her husband says."

Morgan laughed. "Riccardo should be so lucky."

She turned from the mirror. She'd chosen a simple formfitting satin gown to let her lace veil be the showstopper. Flowing from the tiara at the top of her head to ten feet behind her and accented with pearls and sequins, the veil was the epitome of elegance.

Lila clapped. "You look perfect."

Francine walked over and hugged her. "So beautiful."

Paloma, Marguerite and Nanna wiped tears from their eyes. "Such a special day."

The knock at the door had the women scrambling for tissues. "Just a minute."

When Paloma gave the all-clear, Nanna opened the door.

The Colonel began to enter, but seeing his daughter, he stopped. "Oh, my goodness."

Morgan saw the tears in his eyes and she walked over and hugged him. "It's okay."

"No. It's not." He choked back tears. "You look so much like your mother."

She gave Julia a nod and the new mom quietly hustled everyone out of the room.

"You don't often talk about mom."

He pressed his lips together before he drew a long breath. "It's very difficult to lose the love of your life."

"I know. I'd only lost Riccardo for a couple of hours and I thought my life was over. I can't imagine how you felt."

He walked toward a window that looked out

over the garden, where the wedding would be held. "This entire past year, I've been wanting to tell you how proud I am of you."

She laughed. "Really? I thought I'd made the past year difficult."

He pivoted from the window. "No." He winced. "Well, at first, but as everything began to sink in, I realized I hadn't been a very good mom."

Morgan walked over and took his hand. "You've always done the best you could with what you had."

He conceded that with a nod. "I've tried." He caught her gaze. "My mistakes, though, could have really hurt you."

"Nah," she said, batting away his concern. "I think Mom was always looking down on us, making sure you didn't go too far."

He laughed through his tears, then pulled a hanky from the pocket of his perfect black tux.

After wiping his eyes, he took her arm and tucked it in his. "Ready to go marry that Spaniard of yours?"

"Yes." The word came out with glee. She was so full of awe that everything had worked out the way it had that her chest hurt.

He patted her hand. "And you know, of course, I'm expecting grandchildren." He laughed. "Not that I'm telling you what to do."

"Oh, you'll get your grandkids," she assured him. "The Ochoas are all about family."

* * * * *

LET'S TALK

Romance

For exclusive extracts, competitions and special offers, find us online:

- facebook.com/millsandboon
- @millsandboonuk
- @millsandboon

Or get in touch on 0844 844 1351*

For all the latest titles coming soon, visit millsandboon.co.uk/nextmonth

Want even more
ROMANCE?

Join our bookclub today!

'Mills & Boon books, the perfect way to escape for an hour or so.'

Miss W. Dyer

'Excellent service, promptly delivered and very good subscription choices.'

Miss A. Pearson

'You get fantastic special offers and the chance to get books before they hit the shops'

Mrs V. Hall

Visit millsandbook.co.uk/Bookclub and save on brand new books.

MILLS & BOON